TREASURY OF LITERATURE

A Place to Dream

SENIOR AUTHORS
ROGER C. FARR
DOROTHY S. STRICKLAND

AUTHORS
RICHARD F. ABRAHAMSON
ELLEN BOOTH CHURCH
BARBARA BOWEN COULTER
BERNICE E. CULLINAN
MARGARET A. GALLEGO
W. DORSEY HAMMOND
JUDITH L. IRVIN
KAREN KUTIPER
DONNA M. OGLE
TIMOTHY SHANAHAN
PATRICIA SMITH
JUNKO YOKOTA
HALLIE KAY YOPP

SENIOR CONSULTANTS
ASA G. HILLIARD III
JUDY M. WALLIS

CONSULTANTS
ALONZO A. CRIM
ROLANDO R. HINOJOSA-SMITH
LEE BENNETT HOPKINS
ROBERT J. STERNBERG

HARCOURT BRACE & COMPANY

Orlando Atlanta Austin Boston San Francisco Chicago Dallas New York
Toronto London

Acknowledgments

For permission to reprint copyrighted material, grateful acknowledgment is made to the following sources:

Atheneum Publishers, an imprint of Macmillan Publishing Company: Cover illustration by K. Dyble Thompson from *My Name Is María Isabel* by Alma Flor Ada. Illustration copyright © 1993 by K. Dyble Thompson.

Bradbury Press, an Affiliate of Macmillan, Inc.: Cover illustration from *Mozart Tonight* by Julie Downing. Copyright © 1991 by Julie Downing.

Carolrhoda Books, Inc., Minneapolis, MN: Cover illustration by Hannu Taina from *Mister King* by Raija Siekkinen, translated by Tim Steffa. Illustration copyright © 1986 by Hannu Taina.

Crown Publishers, Inc.: Cover illustration from *Elaine, Mary Lewis, and the Frogs* by Heidi Chang. Copyright © 1988 by Heidi Chang.

Dillon Press, Inc.: *A Gift for Tía Rosa* by Karen T. Taha. Text © 1986 by Dillon Press, Inc.

Friends of Henry's and Ramona's Neighborhood: "Henry Huggins' Neighborhood" map by Heather Johnson.

Greenwillow Books, a division of William Morrow & Company, Inc.: *Music, Music for Everyone* by Vera B. Williams. Copyright © 1984 by Vera B. Williams.

Harcourt Brace & Company: Cover illustration from *On the Day You Were Born* by Debra Frasier. Copyright © 1991 by Debra Frasier. *Meet the Orchestra* by Ann Hayes, illustrated by Karmen Thompson. Text copyright © 1991 by Ann Hayes; illustrations copyright © 1991 by Karmen Effenberger Thompson. *Piggins* by Jane Yolen, illustrated by Jane Dyer. Text copyright © 1987 by Jane Yolen; illustrations copyright © 1987 by Jane Dyer. Cover illustration by Jane Dyer from *Picnic with Piggins* by Jane Yolen. Illustration copyright © 1988 by Jane Dyer. Pronunciation Key from *HBJ School Dictionary*, Third Edition. Text copyright © 1990 by Harcourt Brace & Company.

HarperCollins Publishers: "Writers" from *Hey World, Here I Am!* by Jean Little. Text copyright © 1986 by Jean Little. *Through Grandpa's Eyes* by Patricia MacLachlan. Text copyright © 1980 by Patricia MacLachlan. Cover illustration by Pat Cummings from *Storm in the Night* by Mary Stolz. Illustration copyright © 1988 by Pat Cummings.

HarperCollins Publishers Ltd.: Illustrations by Peggy Fortnum from *Paddington* books by Michael Bond.

Holiday House, Inc.: Cover illustration from *Blast Off To Earth! A Look At Geography* by Loreen Leedy. Copyright © 1992 by Loreen Leedy.

Felice Holman: "Who Am I?" from *At the Top of My Voice and Other Poems* by Felice Holman. Text copyright © 1970 by Felice Holman. Published by Charles Scribner's Sons, 1970.

Henry Holt and Company, Inc.: Cover illustration by Vladimir Radunsky from *Hail To Mail* by Samuel Marshak, translated by Richard Pevear. Illustration © 1990 by Vladimir Radunsky.

Houghton Mifflin Company: From "Paddington Paints a Picture" in *Paddington on Stage* by Michael Bond and Alfred Bradley. Text copyright © 1974 by Alfred Bradley and Michael Bond. Based on the play *The Adventures of Paddington Bear*, published by Samuel French Ltd. All rights reserved. *The Lost Lake* by Allen Say. Copyright © 1989 by Allen Say.

International Creative Management, Inc.: "Lisa's Fingerprints" from *Fingers Are Always Bringing Me News* by Mary O'Neill. Text copyright © 1969 by Mary O'Neill. Published by Doubleday, a division of Bantam Doubleday Dell Publishing Group, Inc.

Lothrop, Lee & Shepard Books, a division of William Morrow & Company, Inc.: From *Justin and the Best Biscuits in the World* by Mildred Pitts Walter. Text copyright © 1986 by Mildred Pitts Walter.

Macmillan Publishing Company, a Division of Macmillan, Inc.: "Some People" from *Poems* by Rachel Field. Published by Macmillan Publishing Company, Inc., 1957. Cover illustration from *I Have Another Language: The Language Is Dance* by Eleanor Schick. Copyright © 1992 by Eleanor Schick.

Morrow Junior Books, a division of William Morrow & Company, Inc.: Illustration by Louis Darling from *Ellen Tebbits* by Beverly Cleary. Copyright 1951, 1979 by Beverly Cleary. From "Ramona's Book Report" in *Ramona Quimby, Age 8* by Beverly Cleary, illustrated by Alan Tiegreen. Copyright © 1981 by Beverly Cleary. Cover illustration by Alan Tiegreen from *Ramona Forever* by Beverly Cleary. Illustration copyright © 1984 by William Morrow & Company, Inc. Illustrations by Alan Tiegreen from *The Ramona Quimby Diary* by Beverly Cleary. Illustrations copyright © 1984 by William Morrow & Company, Inc. From *The*

continued on page 335

TREASURY OF LITERATURE

Dear Reader,

Welcome to *A Place to Dream*. A dream can be more than a fanciful picture that you see in your sleep. A dream can also be something that you hope will come true. Making a dream come true can be a challenge.

As you meet the characters in this book, you will see that they also dare to dream, and they work to make their dreams come true. Justin finds out that he can meet challenges. He also learns about famous Black cowboys, who added their own dreams to America's history.

Another dreamer you will meet is Rosa, whose music reminds her neighbors of ways long ago in the "old country." Rosa dreams of helping her family, and she finds a special way to make her dream come true.

Come find your own place to dream among the stories, poems, and articles in this book. Make new friends among the dreamers you meet here. We challenge you to find out how their dreams and yours are alike and how your dreams are different from all others.

Sincerely,
The Authors

UNIT ONE
Being Special / 10

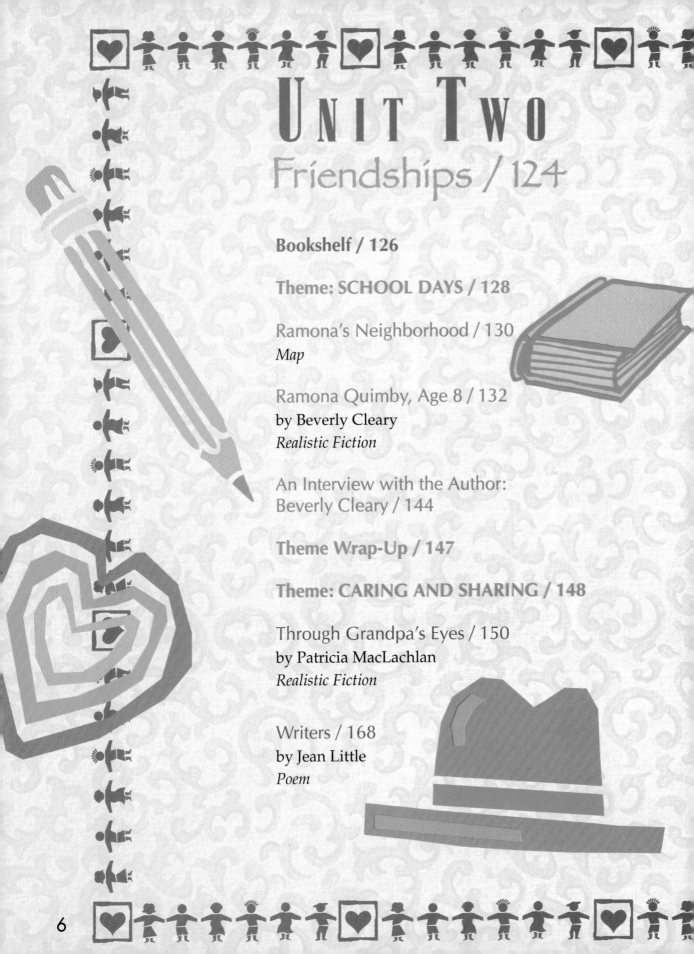

UNIT TWO
Friendships / 124

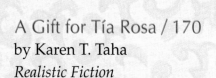

Unit Three
Adventures / 218

UNIT ONE 1

Being Special

People find all kinds of ways to be special. A woman in Kenya plants trees to save her country from becoming a desert. A group of friends start a special band to make music and earn money. As you read these selections, think about the ways you can be special.

THEMES

The Adventures of Ali Baba Bernstein

by Johanna Hurwitz

David Bernstein thinks his life would be more exciting if he had a different name. He changes it to Ali Baba, and guess what! His life does get more exciting.

Children's Choice

Harcourt Brace Library Book

My Name Is María Isabel

by Alma Flor Ada

María Isabel is the new girl in her class. When her teacher insists on calling her Mary, María Isabel has to find a way to show her teacher how important a name can be.

Award-Winning Author

Harcourt Brace Library Book

STORM IN THE NIGHT

by Mary Stolz

When the lights go out during a thunderstorm, Thomas learns more about his grandfather— and about himself.

Teachers' Choice, Coretta Scott King Honor

I HAVE ANOTHER LANGUAGE THE LANGUAGE IS DANCE

by Eleanor Schick

This is the story of one day in the life of a young girl who is a dancer. As she prepares for her first performance in front of an audience, she learns a new language. It is the language of dance.

MOZART TONIGHT

by Julie Downing

In this biography, we ride with Amadeus Mozart and his wife, Constanze, as they travel in a carriage to the opera house. Mozart tells of his struggle to become a composer and of his life with Constanze.

Notable Children's Trade Book in Social Studies

T H E M E

Planting a Seed

Have you ever planted a seed and helped it grow? If you have, you have made the world more beautiful. Read the following selections to see what the characters have done to make their world a better place.

C O N T E N T S

Miss Rumphius

Story and Pictures by BARBARA COONEY

The Lupine Lady lives in a small house overlooking the sea. In between the rocks around her house grow blue and purple and rose-colored flowers. The Lupine Lady is little and old. But she has not always been that way. I know. She is my great-aunt, and she told me so.

Once upon a time she was a little girl named Alice, who lived in a city by the sea. From the front stoop she could see the wharves and the bristling masts of tall ships. Many years ago her grandfather had come to America on a large sailing ship.

Now he worked in the shop at the bottom of the house, making figureheads for the prows of ships, and carving Indians out of wood to put in front of cigar stores. For Alice's grandfather was an artist. He painted pictures, too, of sailing ships and places across the sea. When he was very busy, Alice helped him put in the skies.

In the evening Alice sat on her grandfather's knee and listened to his stories of faraway places. When he had finished, Alice would say, "When I grow up, I too will go to faraway places, and when I grow old, I too will live beside the sea."

"That is all very well, little Alice," said her grandfather, "but there is a third thing you must do."

"What is that?" asked Alice.

"You must do something to make the world more beautiful," said her grandfather.

"All right," said Alice. But she did not know what that could be.

In the meantime Alice got up and washed her face and ate porridge for breakfast. She went to school and came home and did her homework.

And pretty soon she was grown up.

Then my Great-aunt Alice set out to do the three things she had told her grandfather she was going to do. She left home and went to live in another city far from the sea and salt air. There she worked in a library, dusting books and keeping them from getting mixed up, and helping people find the ones they wanted. Some of the books told her about faraway places.

People called her Miss Rumphius now.

Sometimes she went to the conservatory in the middle of the park. When she stepped inside on a wintry day, the warm moist air wrapped itself around her, and the sweet smell of jasmine filled her nose.

"This is almost like a tropical isle," said Miss Rumphius. "But not quite."

So Miss Rumphius went to a real tropical island, where people kept cockatoos and monkeys as pets. She walked on long beaches, picking up beautiful shells. One day she met the Bapa Raja, king of a fishing village.

"You must be tired," he said. "Come into my house and rest."

So Miss Rumphius went in and met the Bapa Raja's wife. The Bapa Raja himself fetched a green coconut and cut a slice off the top so that Miss Rumphius could drink the coconut water inside. Before she left, the Bapa Raja gave her a beautiful mother-of-pearl shell on which he had painted a bird of paradise and the words, "You will always remain in my heart."

"You will always remain in mine too," said Miss Rumphius.

My great-aunt Miss Alice Rumphius climbed tall mountains where the snow never melted. She went through jungles and across deserts. She saw lions playing and kangaroos jumping. And everywhere she made friends she would never forget. Finally she came to the Land of the Lotus-Eaters, and there, getting off a camel, she hurt her back.

"What a foolish thing to do," said Miss Rumphius. "Well, I have certainly seen faraway places. Maybe it is time to find my place by the sea."

And it was, and she did.

From the porch of her new house Miss Rumphius watched the sun come up; she watched it cross the heavens and sparkle on the water; and she saw it set in glory in the evening. She started a little garden among the rocks that surrounded her house, and she planted a few flower seeds in the stony ground. Miss Rumphius was *almost* perfectly happy.

"But there is still one more thing I have to do," she said. "I have to do something to make the world more beautiful."

But what? "The world already is pretty nice," she thought, looking out over the ocean.

24

The next spring Miss Rumphius was not very well. Her back was bothering her again, and she had to stay in bed most of the time.

The flowers she had planted the summer before had come up and bloomed in spite of the stony ground. She could see them from her bedroom window, blue and purple and rose-colored.

"Lupines," said Miss Rumphius with satisfaction. "I have always loved lupines the best. I wish I could plant more seeds this summer so that I could have still more flowers next year."

But she was not able to.

After a hard winter spring came. Miss Rumphius was feeling much better. Now she could take walks again. One afternoon she started to go up and over the hill, where she had not been in a long time.

"I don't believe my eyes!" she cried when she got to the top. For there on the other side of the hill was a large patch of blue and purple and rose-colored lupines!

"It was the wind," she said as she knelt in delight. "It was the wind that brought the seeds from my garden here! And the birds must have helped!"

Then Miss Rumphius had a wonderful idea!

She hurried home and got out her seed catalogues. She sent off to the very best seed house for five bushels of lupine seed.

All that summer Miss Rumphius, her pockets full of seeds, wandered over fields and headlands, sowing lupines. She scattered seeds along the highways and down the country lanes. She flung handfuls of them around the schoolhouse and back of the church. She tossed them into hollows and along stone walls.

Her back didn't hurt her any more at all.

Now some people called her That Crazy Old Lady.

The next spring there were lupines everywhere. Fields and hillsides were covered with blue and purple and rose-colored flowers. They bloomed along the highways and down the lanes. Bright patches lay around the schoolhouse and back of the church. Down in the hollows and along the stone walls grew the beautiful flowers.

Miss Rumphius had done the third, the most difficult thing of all!

My Great-aunt Alice, Miss Rumphius, is very old now. Her hair is very white. Every year there are more and more lupines. Now they call her the Lupine Lady. Sometimes my friends stand with me outside her gate, curious to see the old, old lady who planted the fields of lupines. When she invites us in, they come slowly. They think she is the oldest woman in the world. Often she tells us stories of faraway places.

"When I grow up," I tell her, "I too will go to faraway places and come home to live by the sea."

"That is all very well, little Alice," says my aunt, "but there is a third thing you must do."

"What is that?" I ask.

"You must do something to make the world more beautiful."

"All right," I say.

But I do not know yet

what that can be.

Do you agree with Alice's grandfather that a person should do something to improve the world? Tell why you feel as you do.

Miss Rumphius described her third goal as the most difficult to complete. Why do you think she felt that way?

Besides her grandfather, who or what else was important in Miss Rumphius's life?

WRITE   If you could do something to make the world more beautiful, what would it be? Write a journal entry telling how you would make the world a more beautiful place.

When I was building a house in Maine, I noticed that we had an abundance of lupines on our land. Where did they all come from, I wondered. One of the workmen said, "There's an old woman down in Christmas Cove who goes around throwing lupine seeds. That's why there are so many flowers." I thought that was a good "seed" for a story.

One day, I sat down and said I would write a fairy tale about a heroine who had to do three things, and the hardest was the third, sowing the lupine seeds. The rest of the story patches together things that happened to me or my family. The story starts off in Brooklyn, where I was born, and the travels are mine, though I took them later in my life. My great-grandfather did carve cigar-store Indians, and my grandfather did help him paint in the skies in his pictures. I have ridden on camels, but I don't like them. It's too hard to get on and off!

Knowing I was going to have lots of lupines in my story, the minute they began to bloom I started drawing and photographing them. I didn't finish the book until much later, after the flowers were gone, but at least I had the drawings and the photos to work with.

When I create a book, I always do the story first. I think it's important to have a good story. The pictures come after the story, like beads on a string.

AWARD-WINNING
AUTHOR AND
ILLUSTRATOR

31

A SEED IS A PROMISE

BY CLAIRE MERRILL

You know a lot about seeds.

When you eat an orange, you see little white seeds inside.

You've seen the seeds of other fruits, too—apples, pears, melons, grapes.

Have you eaten peas or lima beans for dinner? Peas and lima beans are seeds. They are the seeds of vegetables.

Have you ever bought flower seed packets in the store? Or fed grass seed to a pet bird?

Have you ever worn maple tree seeds on your nose? Or played tea party with the seeds of an oak tree?

Do you know where all these seeds come from? All seeds come from plants.

And in every seed there is a promise, the promise that a new plant will grow.

If you know what kind of plant a seed comes from, you know what it will grow into.

ILLUSTRATED BY ANDREA EBERBACH

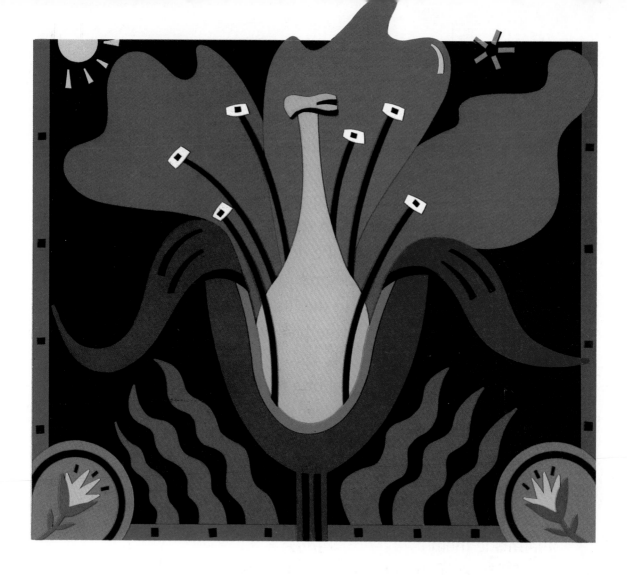

A bean seed will grow into a bean plant. An orange seed will grow into an orange tree. But an orange seed will never grow into a lemon tree.

How are seeds made? Most seeds begin inside flowers. Look at the center part of the flower. This is called the pistil. At the bottom of the pistil there are tiny egg cells.

Now look at the parts around the pistil. These are the stamens. They make a yellow powder called pollen.

A grain of pollen must reach an egg cell to make a seed.

Some flowers use their own pollen to make seeds. But most flowers use the pollen of other flowers.

Bees and other insects carry pollen from flower to flower. Wind blows pollen through the air.

A grain of pollen lands on the pistil of a flower. The pollen grain grows a long tube down into the pistil and joins an egg cell. A seed begins.

Soon the flower starts to die. Its petals dry and fall. The flower dies, but inside the pistil new seeds are growing.

As the seeds grow, a pod or a fruit grows around them. The fruit protects the seeds. The fruit gets bigger and bigger. It gets riper and riper.

The fruit breaks open. The seeds are ready to start new plants.

Some seeds fall to the ground right next to the plant that made them.

Other seeds travel.

The seeds of violets and pansies shoot into the air.

Milkweed and dandelion seeds ride silken strands into the wind.

Some seeds have sturdy wings that let them glide on the wind or float on the water.

Some seeds travel with your help or even with your dog's. Their sharp little burrs hook on to clothing or fur.

Not all of these seeds will grow into plants. Many things may go wrong.

A seed may not land on good earth. It may land on a rock, or in your house. A hungry bird or squirrel may eat it.

But almost every seed starts out with a chance to grow. You can find out why.

Soak a lima bean in water overnight. In the morning, let your mother or father help you cut the seed in half.

Inside you will see a tiny baby plant.

There is a tiny baby plant curled up tight in every seed. This tiny plant can grow into a big plant.

And as long as the tiny plant stays alive, there is a chance that the seed can keep its promise—even after a very long time.

Here is a true story about some seeds that grew after a *very, very* long time.

One day in the cold north country of Canada a miner was digging in the frozen earth.

Deep down, he found some old animal burrows. Inside the burrows were some animal bones. Next to the bones were tiny seeds.

The miner took the bones and seeds. He showed them to some scientists.

The scientists found out that the bones were the bones of little animals called lemmings. The bones were very, very old.

Thousands and thousands of years ago, in prehistoric times, the lemmings must have stored the seeds for food.

Everyone wondered, could such old seeds still grow? Had the earth acted like the freezer in your refrigerator? Had it kept the seeds from spoiling?

The scientists put the seeds on special wet paper and waited.

Two days later, this is what they saw. Some of the seeds had kept their promise. They had sprouted after thousands and thousands of years.

In time the seeds grew into healthy plants. The plants grew flowers. The flowers made new seeds—each with a promise of its own.

What did you learn by reading "A Seed Is a Promise"?

In what ways is a seed like a promise?

WRITE   Write a description of a flower. Try to add details in your description that will help your reader to see it.

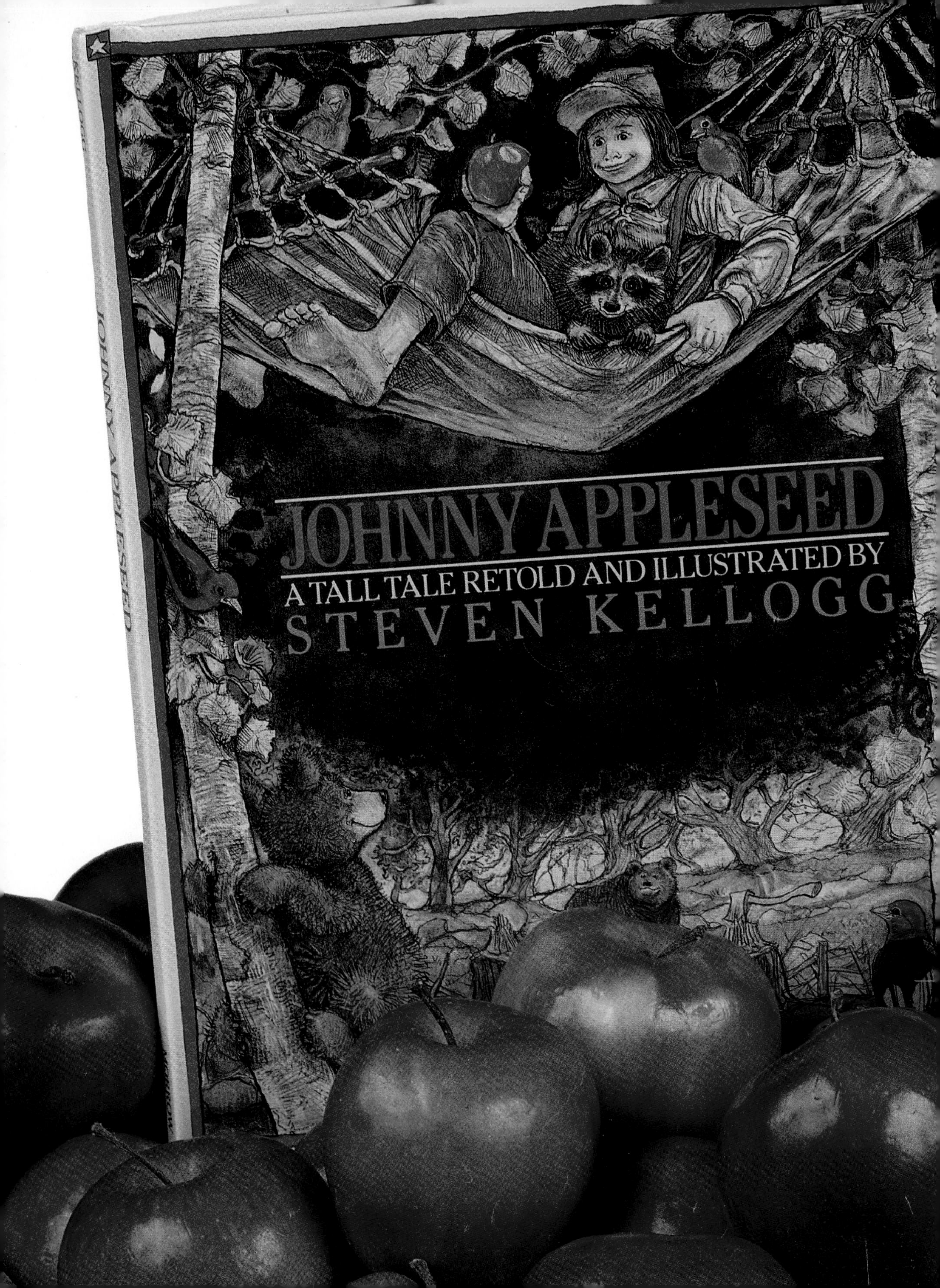

JOHNNY APPLESEED
A TALL TALE RETOLD AND ILLUSTRATED BY
STEVEN KELLOGG
KELLOGG
JOHNNY APPLESEED

John Chapman, who later became known as Johnny Appleseed, was born on September 26, 1774, when the apples on the trees surrounding his home in Leominster, Massachusetts, were as red as the autumn leaves.

John's first years were hard. His father left the family to fight in the Revolutionary War, and his mother and his baby brother both died before his second birthday.

By the time John turned six, his father had remarried and settled in Longmeadow, Massachusetts. Within a decade their little house was overflowing with ten more children.

Nearby was an apple orchard. Like most early American families, the Chapmans picked their apples in the fall, stored them in the cellar for winter eating, and used them to make sauces, cider, vinegar, and apple butter. John loved to watch spring blossoms slowly turn into the glowing fruit of autumn.

Watching the apples grow inspired in John a love of all of nature. He often escaped from his boisterous household to the tranquil woods. The animals sensed his gentleness and trusted him.

As soon as John was old enough to leave home, he set out to explore the vast wilderness to the west. When he reached the Allegheny Mountains, he cleared a plot of land and planted a small orchard with the pouch of apple seeds he had carried with him.

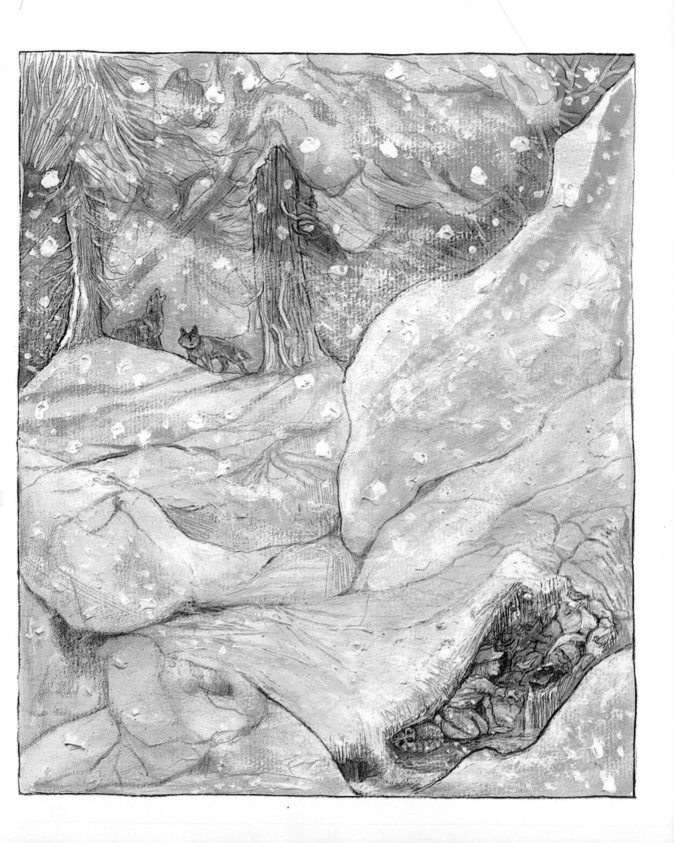

John walked hundreds of miles through the Pennsylvania forest, living like the Indians he befriended on the trail. As he traveled, he cleared the land for many more orchards. He was sure the pioneer families would be arriving before long, and he looked forward to supplying them with apple trees.

When a storm struck, he found shelter in a hollow log or built a lean-to. On clear nights he stretched out under the stars.

Over the next few years, John continued to visit and care for his new orchards. The winters slowed him down, but he survived happily on a diet of butternuts.

One spring he met a band of men who boasted that they could lick their weight in wildcats. They were amazed to hear that John wouldn't hurt an animal and had no use for a gun.

They challenged John to compete at wrestling, the favorite frontier sport. He suggested a more practical contest—a tree-chopping match. The woodsmen eagerly agreed.

When the sawdust settled, there was no question
about who had come out on top.

John was pleased that the land for his largest orchard had been so quickly cleared. He thanked the exhausted woodsmen for their help and began planting.

During the next few years, John continued to move westward. Whenever he ran out of apple seeds, he hiked to the eastern cider presses to replenish his supply. Before long, John's plantings were spread across the state of Ohio.

Meanwhile, pioneer families were arriving in search of homesites and farmland. John had located his orchards on the routes he thought they'd be traveling. As he had hoped, the settlers were eager to buy his young trees.

John went out of his way to lend a helping hand to his new neighbors. Often he would give his trees away. People affectionately called him Johnny Appleseed, and he began using that name.

He particularly enjoyed entertaining children with tales of his wilderness adventures and stories from the Bible.

In 1812 the British incited the Indians to join them in another war against the Americans. The settlers feared that Ohio would be invaded from Lake Erie.

It grieved Johnny that his friends were fighting each other. But when he saw the smoke of burning cabins, he ran through the night, shouting a warning at every door.

After the war, people urged Johnny to build a
house and settle down. He replied that he lived like a
king in his wilderness home, and he returned to the
forest he loved.

During his long absences, folks enjoyed sharing
their recollections of Johnny. They retold his stories
and sometimes they even exaggerated them a bit.

Some recalled Johnny sleeping in a treetop hammock and chatting with the birds.

Others remembered that a rattlesnake had attacked his foot. Fortunately, Johnny's feet were as tough as elephant's hide, so the fangs didn't penetrate.

It was said that Johnny had once tended a wounded wolf and then kept him for a pet.

An old hunter swore he'd seen Johnny frolicking with a bear family.

The storytellers outdid each other with tall tales about his feats of survival in the untamed wilderness.

As the years passed, Ohio became too crowded for Johnny. He moved to the wilds of Indiana, where he continued to clear land for his orchards.

When the settlers began arriving, Johnny recognized some of the children who had listened to his stories. Now they had children of their own.

It made Johnny's old heart glad when they welcomed him as a beloved friend and asked to hear his tales again.

When Johnny passed seventy, it became difficult for him to keep up with his work. Then, in March of 1845, while trudging through a snowstorm near Fort Wayne, Indiana, he became ill for the first time in his life.

Johnny asked for shelter in a settler's cabin, and a few days later he died there.

Curiously, Johnny's stories continued to move westward without him. Folks maintained that they'd seen him in Illinois or that he'd greeted them in Missouri, Arkansas, or Texas. Others were certain that he'd planted trees on the slopes of the Rocky Mountains or in California's distant valleys.

Even today people still claim they've seen Johnny Appleseed.

Are you like Johnny Appleseed in any way? Why or why not?

How did Johnny Appleseed help to settle the West?

A folk hero is an everyday person who becomes famous. How does Johnny Appleseed fit that description?

WRITE   Imagine you are Johnny Appleseed, moving from place to place planting apples. Write a newspaper story about your travels. Begin when you first leave home, and stop when you leave Ohio.

Planting a Seed

Johnny Appleseed planted apple trees far and wide. Miss Rumphius planted flowers at home. If you wanted to do something to make the world more beautiful, would you start in your own neighborhood? Or would you go far from home to begin? Tell why you feel as you do.

WRITER'S WORKSHOP

Think about a time when something you did made someone happy. Write a paragraph describing what you did and how you felt before and after.

Writer's Choice:
You have read about people who did special things. You might want to write about something special you could do. Plan what you will write, and carry out your plan.

THEME

Being Different

Are you glad to be different from everyone else? As you read the following story and poems, think about the ways each person is different and special, even when he or she seems ordinary in other ways.

CONTENTS

55

CHILDREN'S CHOICE

BY JOHANNA HURWITZ
ILLUSTRATED BY JAN PALMER

 avid Bernstein was eight years, five months, and seventeen days old when he chose his new name.

There were already four Davids in David Bernstein's third-grade class. Every time his teacher, Mrs. Booxbaum, called, "David," all four boys answered. David didn't like that one bit. He wished he had an exciting name like one of the explorers he learned about in social studies—Vasco Da Gama. Once he found two unusual names on a program his parents brought home from a concert—Zubin Mehta and Wolfgang Amadeus Mozart. Now those were names with pizzazz!

David Bernstein might have gone along forever being just another David if it had not been for the book report that his teacher assigned.

"I will give extra credit for fat books," Mrs. Booxbaum told the class.

She didn't realize that all of her students would try to outdo one another. That afternoon when the third grade went to the school library, everyone tried to find the fattest book.

Melanie found a book with eighty pages.

Sam found a book with ninety-seven pages.

Jeffrey found a book with one hundred nineteen pages.

David K. and David S. each took a copy of the same book. It had one hundred forty-five pages.

None of the books were long enough for David Bernstein. He looked at a few that had over one hundred pages. He found one that had two hundred fourteen pages. But he wanted a book that had more pages than the total of all the pages in all the books his classmates were reading. He wanted to be the best student in the class—even in the entire school.

That afternoon he asked his mother what the fattest book was. Mrs. Bernstein thought for a minute. "I guess that would have to be the Manhattan telephone book," she said.

David Bernstein rushed to get the phone book. He lifted it up and opened to the last page. When he saw that it had over 1,578 pages, he was delighted.

He knew that no student in the history of P.S. 35 had ever read such a fat book. Just think how much extra credit he would get! David took the book and began to read name after name after name. After turning through all the *A* pages, he skipped to the name Bernstein. He found the listing for his father, Robert Bernstein. There were fifteen of them. Then he counted the number of David Bernsteins in the telephone book. There were seventeen. There was also a woman named Davida and a man named Davis, but he didn't count them. Right at that moment, David Bernstein decided two things: he would change his name and he would find another book to read.

The next day David went back to the school library. He asked the librarian to help him pick out a very fat book. "But it must be very exciting, too," he told her.

"I know just the thing for you," said the librarian.

She handed David a thick book with a bright

red cover. It was *The Arabian Nights.* It had only three hundred thirty-seven pages, but it looked a lot more interesting than the phone book. David checked the book out of the library and spent the entire evening reading it. When he showed the book to his teacher the next day, she was very pleased.

"That is a good book," she said. "David, you have made a fine choice."

It was at that moment that David Bernstein announced his new name. He had found it in the library book.

"From now on," David said, "I want to be called Ali Baba Bernstein."

Mrs. Booxbaum was surprised. David's parents were even more surprised. "David is a beautiful name," said his mother. "It was my grandfather's name."

"You can't just go around changing your name when you feel like it," his father said. "How will I ever know who I'm talking to?"

"You'll know it's still me," Ali Baba told his parents.

Mr. and Mrs. Bernstein finally agreed, although both of them frequently forgot and called their son David.

So now in Mrs. Booxbaum's class, there were three Davids and one Ali Baba. Ali Baba Bernstein was very happy. He was sure that a boy with an exciting name would have truly exciting adventures.

Only time would tell.

he first Ali Baba—the one Ali Baba Bernstein had read about in his library book—found a robber's treasure. He knew the magic words to open a secret cave and he knew how to trick the wicked robbers. Nothing like that ever happened to Ali Baba Bernstein. Five days a week he went to school. Third grade was not very different from second grade, even if the work was a little harder. The kids were the same and the games they played at recess or in phys ed were about the same, too.

Sometimes on the weekends Ali Baba rode the subway to his grandparents' house. As the train rumbled along and the lights in the dark tunnel flickered on and off, Ali Baba would pretend the train had crossed onto a secret track. Maybe they were all heading to a mysterious cave deep underground where robbers had hidden gold and jewels. The speeding train would begin to slow down as it approached a station. Ali Baba hoped it would be a station where no train had ever stopped before. But then he looked out the train window. The sign read: SIXTY-SIXTH STREET, where his grandparents lived.

"I thought having a name like Ali Baba would make things pick up around here," Ali Baba complained to his mother. "But I still keep doing David sort of things."

"Changing your name won't make your life any

different," Mrs. Bernstein said. "It won't make you grow up any faster. This year you can cross Broadway by yourself," his mother reminded him. "You can walk to Roger Zucker's house all alone. Last year you thought that was a big deal."

It was true. A year ago, crossing Broadway, a two-way street with lots of traffic, *had* seemed like a big

adventure. Now that he could actually do it, Ali Baba longed for bigger adventures than just crossing the street.

One Saturday morning when Ali Baba Bernstein was eight years, six months, and twenty-three days old, his mother asked him to help her carry the laundry down to the basement of their apartment building, where there were washing machines and dryers.

Mrs. Bernstein began to load two of the machines with laundry, but she realized that she'd forgotten the detergent.

"David, will you watch our laundry while I go get the soap?"

"My name is Ali Baba," he corrected her. "Don't worry about the laundry." Who in the world would want to steal their dirty clothes?

Mrs. Bernstein went to the elevator and Ali Baba sat down near the washing machines. But after a moment or two he got up and started to look around. The dim, slightly damp basement was a little like a cave, he thought.

In one corner of the basement was the furnace that heated the building during the winter and made the hot water. Ali Baba could hear the furnace's motor and the whole area around it was hot. It didn't exactly frighten him, but he decided he would rather explore another part of the basement instead. This was where people in the building stored their old furniture, bikes, baby carriages, suitcases, and anything else that they didn't need but didn't want to get rid of.

The storage area was divided into cages with heavy mesh wiring between each cage. Ali Baba had been inside the cage where the Bernsteins kept their castoffs. He peeked in now and tried the door to the cage but it was locked. Through the wire mesh, he could see his old tricycle from when he was little and even his crib, which stood in pieces leaning against someone else's table.

Ali Baba walked down the row of cages, trying each door as he went past. He didn't expect any of the doors to be open, but he tried anyway. At the very end of the row, he found one door that was unlocked. He went inside.

There were old chairs covered with dusty velvet and three big, old-fashioned trunks, like the ones Ali Baba had seen in movies. He didn't know anyone who owned anything like them. It didn't seem like snooping to open them, especially when the lids on the trunks lifted so easily. Ali Baba wrinkled his nose at the odor of mothballs. The first two trunks contained old clothing. He almost didn't open the third trunk. But he knew the first

Ali Baba would never leave a trunk unexplored so he decided to take a peek. Even in the dim light, he had no trouble seeing what was in the third trunk. It was filled with sparkling diamonds, rubies, pearls, and gold chains.

Ali Baba could hardly believe his eyes. He closed the lid and read the label with the owner's name: VIVALDI. Who was that?

"David, David," a voice called. It was his mother returning to the basement with the soap. Ali Baba was so stunned by what he had found in the third trunk that he didn't even correct her when she used his old name. All he could think about was the jewels. He was about to tell his mother everything but he stopped just in time. She might say that he had no business poking into other people's trunks.

At lunchtime, Ali Baba was still wondering about the jewels. Why would anyone keep a treasure in the basement? It must be that the owner of the jewels did not want anyone to find them inside his apartment. The more he thought about it, the more certain he was that he had stumbled on a stolen treasure. He wished he could talk about this with his friend Roger Zucker. Maybe the two of them could solve the mystery together. Unfortunately Roger and his family had gone away for the weekend. Ali Baba would have to get to the bottom of this mystery by himself. He would make sure the jewels were returned to their rightful owners. He would be a hero just like the first Ali Baba!

After lunch, Ali Baba's mother asked him to go get the mail. Although there was rarely any mail for him, this was a chore Ali Baba enjoyed. Today he studied all the names on all the other mail boxes in the lobby. Box 4K was labeled VIVALDI. There was no question about it. The thief lived right in this building!

"Did you ever hear the name Vivaldi?" Ali Baba asked his parents when he returned with the mail.

"Of course," said his mother. "He's an Italian composer of baroque music."

"Does he have a police record?" asked Ali Baba.

"Not that I know of. He's been dead at least two hundred years."

"I don't think we're talking about the same man," said Ali Baba. The jewels in the basement couldn't have been there that long. The building was only fifty years old.

"There's someone named Vivaldi living in this building," said Mr. Bernstein, looking up from the letter he was reading. "I met him at a tenants' meeting. He was worried that he wouldn't be able to buy his apartment if our building was turned into a co-op. I told him that as a senior citizen he couldn't be evicted."

A thief should be evicted, Ali Baba thought darkly. But he didn't say anything.

That afternoon Mrs. Bernstein sent Ali Baba to the store on the corner. She needed eggs for a recipe she wanted to try. Ali Baba was glad to go. On the way back he could check up on Mr. Vivaldi. Ali Baba rode the elevator down to the street and rushed to get the eggs. When he returned to the building, he got off the elevator at the fourth floor.

Even as he was coming out of the elevator, Ali Baba could hear a woman screaming. As he approached the door of 4K, he heard the woman's screams come from inside the apartment. Ali Baba stood frozen. Did Mr. Vivaldi lure women with jewels into his apartment and rob them? The woman screamed again.

Why couldn't any of Mr. Vivaldi's neighbors hear her? The woman shrieked louder. Without thinking, Ali Baba banged on Mr. Vivaldi's door. He didn't have any weapon on him. All he had was a dozen eggs. If he had to, he could throw them at Mr. Vivaldi.

"Open the door!" shouted Ali Baba.

Slowly the apartment door opened. Ali Baba was about to rush inside, but one look at the man in the doorway stopped him.

He had on a helmet, but it didn't look like the kind football players wore. He was holding a shield, and there was a sword hanging from his waist.

The woman shrieked again. Ali Baba remembered why he was there. "I'll save you," Ali Baba cried and pushed his way into the apartment. He could hear the woman, but he couldn't see her.

"Where did you hide her?" Ali Baba demanded. He pulled the carton of eggs out of the paper bag. If Mr. Vivaldi drew his sword, he would throw it in his face.

"Is she in the bathroom?"

"What's wrong with you, young man?" asked Mr. Vivaldi.

"What's wrong with *me*?" Ali Baba said. "You're the one who steals women's jewels. Shame on you. You should be in jail."

Mr. Vivaldi walked over to his phonograph and turned it off. Suddenly the room was quiet. There was no more shrieking.

"Who are you?" asked the man. "Will you please tell me what this is all about?"

Ali Baba held the carton of eggs ready, just in case. "I heard a woman screaming in here," he said. "I want to know where she is."

"I think you mean *Norma*," said the man.

"Aha!" said Ali Baba. "I knew it. Don't try any of your tricks."

"*Norma* is the name of an opera. The role was sung by Maria Callas."

"Maria?" echoed Ali Baba. "How many women do

you have stashed in this apartment?"

"Alas," sighed Mr. Vivaldi. "Maria Callas is dead. It is a great loss to the world."

"You should have thought of that before you killed her," Ali Baba said. "Don't make a move, or I'll throw these eggs at you. I'm going to call the police."

Ali Baba edged toward the telephone. He remembered that the number for emergencies was 911.

"I didn't kill her," said Mr. Vivaldi. "That was a role I never got."

"Then who did?" demanded Ali Baba. "Do you have an accomplice? And where did you get all those jewels I saw in the basement?"

Mr. Vivaldi sat down on his sofa. "I'm sorry. I think there has been a misunderstanding," he said.

"It's too late for excuses, Mr. Vivaldi."

"Please," the man said. "Put down those eggs before you drop them on my carpet. I'll tell you everything."

Reluctantly Ali Baba put down the eggs. If Mr. Vivaldi lunged forward with his sword, Ali Baba would have to move very quickly.

"For many years I sang with the opera," said Mr. Vivaldi. "I had many fine roles. Now I am too old to sing onstage. But I still listen to my operas on the phonograph. I like to pretend that I'm singing before an audience. That's why I've kept my old costumes."

"I didn't think you bought that outfit at a department store," said Ali Baba.

Mr. Vivaldi smiled. "You heard me playing the opera *Norma*. To you, I guess, it did sound like someone screaming. But what you actually heard was the voice of Maria Callas."

"The one who's dead?" asked Ali Baba.

Mr. Vivaldi nodded.

"Then there aren't any women in the apartment with

you?" Ali Baba didn't know if he was relieved or disappointed.

"That is correct, young man."

"But what about the jewels?" asked Ali Baba. "I saw them with my own eyes in the trunk in the basement. Who did you steal them from?"

"I think you are referring to the fake jewelry we used on the stage," said Mr. Vivaldi. "Alas, none of it is worth a penny."

"You mean those aren't real diamonds and rubies?"

Mr. Vivaldi shook his head.

"Gee," said Ali Baba. "I never saw so many jewels before. I was sure you were a robber." He looked the old man straight in the eye. "Are you sure you aren't lying to me?"

"Young man," said Mr. Vivaldi, "you flatter me. Imagine thinking I was young enough to be a jewel thief. You make me feel seventy again! And I'm going to be eighty-three on my next birthday."

"Gee," said Ali Baba. "That's really old."

"So it is," said Mr. Vivaldi. "How old are you?"

"Eight years, six months, and twenty-three days," said Ali Baba.

"That's a good age," said Mr. Vivaldi. "What is your name? You never told me."

"Ali Baba. Ali Baba Bernstein."

"Interesting name. Well, Ali Baba, now that we are properly introduced, come another day if you would like. We can listen to *Carmen* together."

Ali Baba got ready to leave. He knew his mother would be wondering where he was.

As he waited for the elevator, Ali Baba could hear the phonograph playing again in apartment 4K. This time a man was singing. Ali Baba wondered if that was the way Mr. Vivaldi used to sound. He stood listening to the music until the elevator came.

If you could change your name, what name would you choose? Explain why.

How do David's parents feel about him changing his name?

What do you think Ali Baba learns in this story?

WRITE After David changes his name to Ali Baba, he seems to look for adventure. Make a list of how you think your life would change if you had a different name.

Words from the Author:
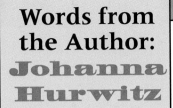
Johanna Hurwitz

When I write a book, I seldom think of the title first. With *The Adventures of Ali Baba Bernstein,* it was the name that bounced into my head. I remembered that when my son was young, the name David was very popular, and at one time there were four Davids in his class. I decided to write about a boy who changes his name.

Sometimes I use things that happened to my children as a starting point for a story. When my first book came out, the characters I was writing about, Busybody Nora and her brother, Teddy, were 5 and 3, and my children were 10 and 12. Because Nora and Teddy were so young, my children didn't feel as if I was talking about them.

I always wanted to be a writer, but I never really knew I was a funny writer until after my first book was done. It surprised me. Sometimes I look at my stuff and say, "Hey, I wrote that! It's funny!" I guess the way I write fits in with my philosophy of life—you'd better laugh at things, or otherwise you'll be crying much of the time.

AWARD-WINNING
AUTHOR

Lisa's Fingerprints

by Mary O'Neill

Some say I have my mother's nose,
My father's eyes, my uncle's toes,
And so I think it is just fine
My fingerprints are only mine.
Not my father, or my mother,
Or my sister or my brother,
Those now, before, or after me
Will lack this nonconformity.
No set of prints whose every line
Matches yours, or matches mine.
Is this distinction true within
The world of wing, paw, hoof, and fin?

Who Am I?

by Felice Holman
illustrated by Karen Barbour

The trees ask me,
And the sky,
And the sea asks me
Who am I?

The grass asks me,
And the sand,
And the rocks ask me
Who I am.

The wind tells me
At nightfall,
And the rain tells me
Someone small.

Someone small
Someone small
But a piece
of
it
all.

Being Different

Ali Baba Bernstein, Lisa, and the author of "Who Am I?" all want you to see just how different they are. Ali Baba even changes his name to be different. Do you think a new name or a nickname could make you act a certain way? Explain why you think as you do.

WRITER'S WORKSHOP

Write a paragraph about yourself. Give details that tell how you are special.

Writer's Choice: You might want to write about the ways in which people are the same instead of how they are different. Choose an idea, and write about it. Share your idea.

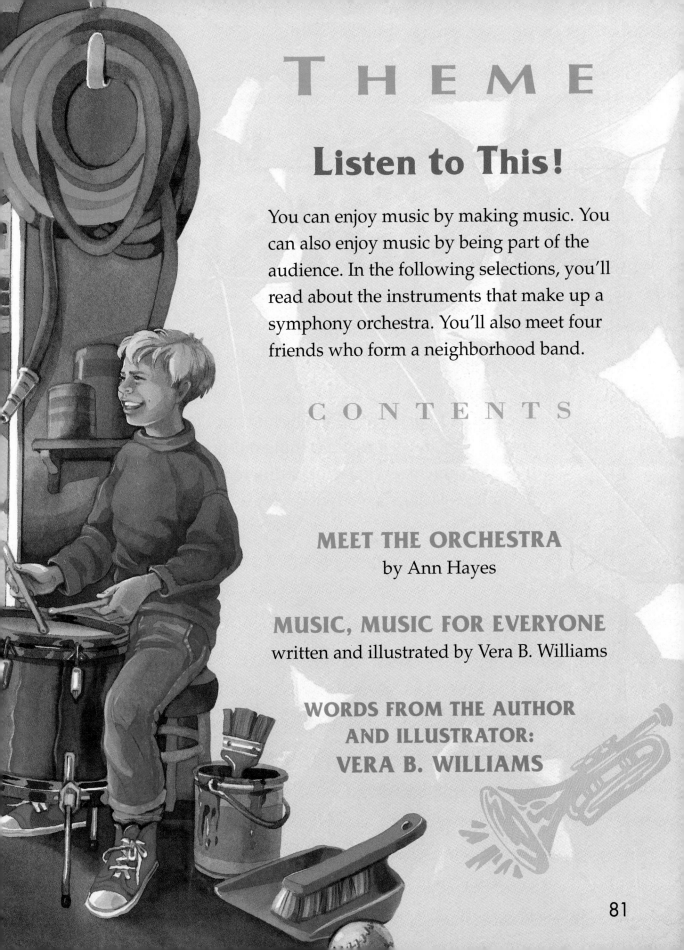

THEME

Listen to This!

You can enjoy music by making music. You can also enjoy music by being part of the audience. In the following selections, you'll read about the instruments that make up a symphony orchestra. You'll also meet four friends who form a neighborhood band.

CONTENTS

Meet the Orchestra

written by Ann Hayes

illustrated by Karmen Thompson

The orchestra plays tonight. The audience has arrived. The musicians are coming on stage with their instruments. What a lot of different kinds they play—strings, woodwinds, brass, and percussion.

Violin

Players with like instruments sit together in "families." The violin belongs to the string family, along with the viola, the cello, and the big string bass. You play all of these with a bow or pluck them with your fingers. The violin is the smallest of the string instruments. Its song can be bright as laughter, light as air, soft as a whisper, or sad as a tear.

Viola

As instruments get bigger, their voices get lower. The viola looks and sounds like a big brother to the violin. It has a deeper tone, reminding you of evening shadows, cloudy skies, and the color blue.

83

Cello

You can't tuck a cello under your chin the way you do a violin or viola. It is so big you must rest it on the floor. The cello's rich, mellow voice speaks of deep feelings like joy and sadness. It can remind you of the calm beauty of a drifting swan and of the color purple.

String Bass

The string bass is the grandpapa of the string family. It is so tall that you must stand up or sit on a high stool to play it. When bowed, its low notes moan and groan. When plucked, its booming sound helps other musicians to keep the beat.

Flute

The flute belongs to the woodwind family, along with the
piccolo, oboe, bassoon, and clarinet. You blow into these
instruments to play them. At one time, all of them
were made of wood; today the flute is often
made of silver or even of gold.
To play the flute, you hold it sideways,
tighten your lips,
and blow across the air hole.
With practice, you can trill like
a bird or play slow, quivering
notes as cool as a mountain
stream.

Piccolo

The piccolo, little sister to the
flute, loves attention and always
gets it. This tiny flute is so shrill you
can't help hearing it. Its high notes
almost pierce your eardrums. Yet
everyone loves the piccolo
because it has such a
great sense of fun.

Oboe

The oboe has a mouthpiece made of reed. The reed can be fussy and troublesome. Then it honks like a goose with a bad cold.

But usually the oboe can be trusted. The oboe plays that single note to which the whole orchestra tunes 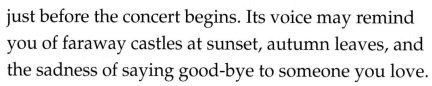 just before the concert begins. Its voice may remind you of faraway castles at sunset, autumn leaves, and the sadness of saying good-bye to someone you love.

Bassoon

The bassoon is like a large, folded oboe. It also has a reed mouthpiece. Its voice, like its name, has a kind of loneliness. Yet the bassoon can also be playful. It chats and chuckles with the other instruments. You often hear it chugging along like a tough little engine. Can't you almost see puffs of smoke coming out the top?

Clarinet

Here are two different clarinets.
The straight one is nimble and quick.
It tootles up and down the scale, never tripping
over a note. Its cool tones melt in your ears
just like ice cream melts in your mouth.

This very long clarinet is bent at both ends
so that it doesn't touch the floor when played.
Its low, slow notes may remind you of clouds
drifting across the moon or a snake swaying
to a snake charmer's music.

B-flat clarinet

bass clarinet

French Horn

Make way for the brass family, the powerhouse of the orchestra! Even when they play softly, you can sense a huge cat crouched to spring.

The brass do not have reed mouthpieces. Your lips buzzing against the metal mouthpiece produce the sound. The tubes of the horns magnify it, as a bullhorn magnifies an announcer's voice.

The French horn is like a big, bright bell at the end of a long, thin tube. The tube is coiled, so the horn can be played with one hand on the valves and the other inside the bell. The hand inside softens the sound. (Uncoiled, the French horn would reach all the way across a very large room. Someone would surely trip over it.)

The French horn has many voices. It can calm you with its gentle tones or thrill you with its gallant hunting call.

Trumpet

The trumpet's shorter tube makes it look easier to play than some of the fancier brass. But is it? No, say the trumpeters. You must work just as hard to learn it.

The trumpet's call is noble and exciting. It can remind you of flags flying, soldiers marching, and royal persons entering a great hall.

Tuba

The tuba has a huge bell and a very long tube. Do you remember that the bigger strings have deeper voices? The same is true of the horns. The bigger ones make lower sounds.

The tuba seldom carries a tune. It is more of a rhythm instrument. Its "umpahs" help the brass to keep the beat, just as the thump of the bass does for the strings.

Timpani or Kettledrums

The big kettledrums sit in the "kitchen," or percussion section of the orchestra. Everything that is beaten, banged, dinged, or pinged belongs there.

Have you ever heard the orchestra rumble with the sound of distant thunder? Suddenly it explodes with a "BOOM-BOOM-BOOM!" That is the timpani. They look like big kettles sitting side by side. Each has a slightly different pitch. You beat rapidly from one to another, making the thunder crash and roll.

Cymbals

The cymbals look like a pair of pot lids. When banged together, they crash with the fury of an electric storm. If the kettledrums give you the roll of thunder, the cymbals give you the flash of lightning. Hear them ring out just when the music reaches a peak of excitement. This is a proud moment for the whole orchestra!

Piano

When you sit down at the piano, the black and white keys make your fingers want to dance. From the center you can play them all—the high ones on your right and the low ones on your left.

When you hear a murmur of notes burst into thundering chords, then fade into silence, it is probably the voice of the piano. When it is over, you may want to clap—or perhaps even cry.

Conductor

Now, meet the conductor. He is often called "maestro," which means master of the orchestra. That he is, for he leads the musicians at all times. He does it mostly by talking with his hands! In his right hand he holds a small stick—the baton. With it he beats time. His left hand motions, "You play now!" "Be quick!" "Livelier!"

"Louder!" "Softer!" "Ah, that's perfect!" A raised eyebrow says, "You're playing off key!"

The musicians have taken their places. The strings, who are by far the largest group of players, sit in front, almost filling the stage. The woodwinds sit close together at the center. The brass and percussion are in back.

The conductor strides on stage in front of the orchestra, raises his baton . . .

Let the music start!

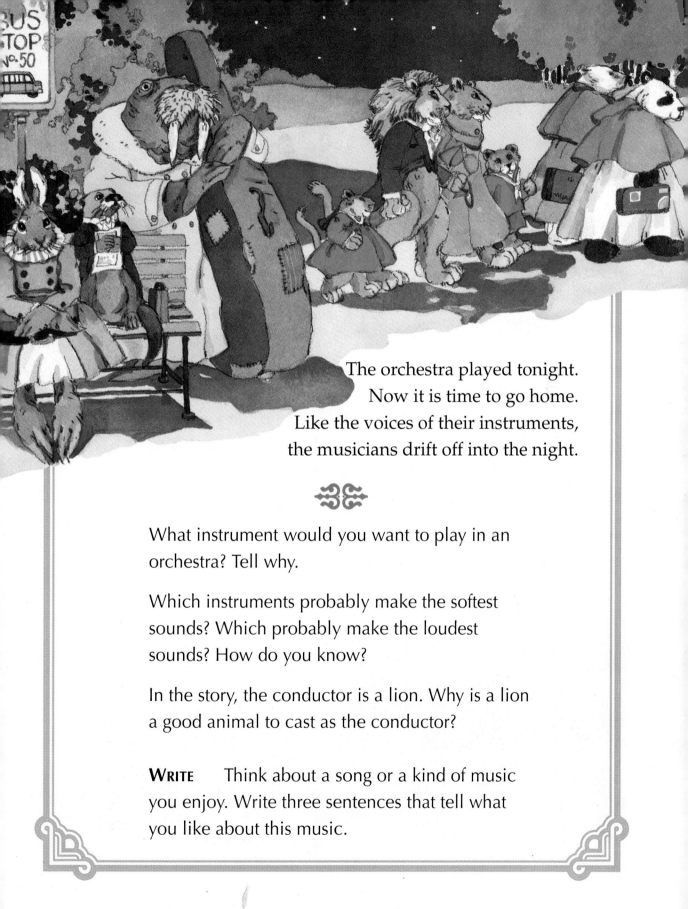

The orchestra played tonight.
Now it is time to go home.
Like the voices of their instruments,
the musicians drift off into the night.

What instrument would you want to play in an orchestra? Tell why.

Which instruments probably make the softest sounds? Which probably make the loudest sounds? How do you know?

In the story, the conductor is a lion. Why is a lion a good animal to cast as the conductor?

WRITE   Think about a song or a kind of music you enjoy. Write three sentences that tell what you like about this music.

MUSIC, MUSIC FOR EVERYONE
VERA B. WILLIAMS

Our big chair often sits in our living room empty now.

When I first got my accordion, Grandma and Mama used to sit in that chair together to listen to me practice. And every day after school while Mama was at her job at the diner, Grandma would be sitting in the chair by the window. Even if it was snowing big flakes down on her hair, she would lean way out to call, "Hurry up, Pussycat. I've got something nice for you."

But now Grandma is sick. She has to stay upstairs in the big bed in Aunt Ida and Uncle Sandy's extra room. Mama and Aunt Ida and Uncle Sandy and I take turns taking care of her.

When I come home from school, I run right upstairs to ask Grandma if she wants anything.

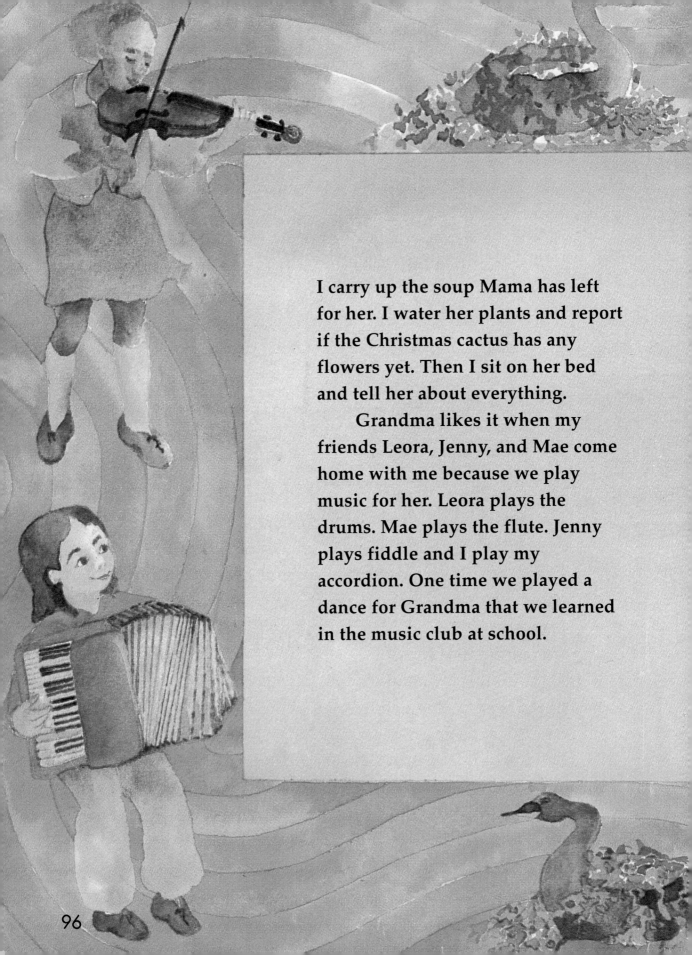

I carry up the soup Mama has left for her. I water her plants and report if the Christmas cactus has any flowers yet. Then I sit on her bed and tell her about everything.

Grandma likes it when my friends Leora, Jenny, and Mae come home with me because we play music for her. Leora plays the drums. Mae plays the flute. Jenny plays fiddle and I play my accordion. One time we played a dance for Grandma that we learned in the music club at school.

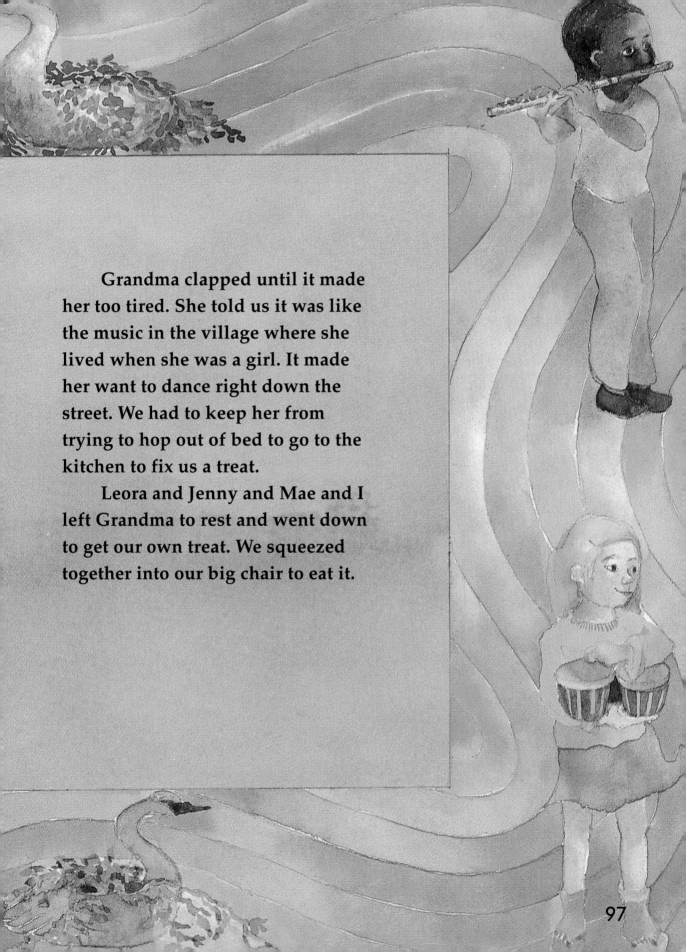

Grandma clapped until it made her too tired. She told us it was like the music in the village where she lived when she was a girl. It made her want to dance right down the street. We had to keep her from trying to hop out of bed to go to the kitchen to fix us a treat.

Leora and Jenny and Mae and I left Grandma to rest and went down to get our own treat. We squeezed together into our big chair to eat it.

"It feels sad down here without your grandma," Leora said. "Even your big money jar up there looks sad and empty."

"Remember how it was full to the top and I couldn't even lift it when we bought the chair for my mother?" I said.

"And remember how it was more than half full when you got your accordion?" Jenny said.

"I bet it's empty now because your mother has to spend all her money to take care of your grandma till she gets better. That's how it was when my father had his accident and couldn't go to work for a long time," Mae said.

Mae had a dime in her pocket and she dropped it into the jar. "That will make it look a little fuller anyway," she said as she went home.

But after Jenny and Leora and Mae went home, our jar looked even emptier to me. I wondered how we would ever be able to fill it up again while Grandma was sick. I wondered when Grandma would be able to come downstairs again. Even our beautiful chair with roses all over it seemed empty with just me in the corner of it. The whole house seemed so empty and so quiet.

I got out my accordion and I started to play.
The notes sounded beautiful in the empty room.
One song that is an old tune sounded so pretty I
played it over and over. I remembered what my
mother had told me about my other grandma and
how she used to play the accordion. Even when she
was a girl not much bigger than I, she would get up
and play at a party or a wedding so the company
could dance and sing. Then people would stamp
their feet and yell, "More, more!" When they went
home, they would leave money on the table for her.

That's how I got an idea for how I could help
fill up the jar again. I ran right upstairs.
"Grandma," I whispered. "Grandma?"

"Is that you, Pussycat?" she answered in a
sleepy voice. "I was just having such a nice dream
about you. Then I woke up and heard you playing
that beautiful old song. Come. Sit here and brush
my hair."

I brushed Grandma's hair and told her my
whole idea. She thought it was a great idea. "But
tell the truth, Grandma," I begged her. "Do you
think kids could really do that?"

"I think you and Jenny and Leora and Mae could do it. No question. No question at all," she answered. "Only don't wait a minute to talk to them about it. Go call and ask them now."

And that was how the Oak Street Band got started.

Our music teachers helped us pick out pieces we could all play together. Aunt Ida, who plays guitar, helped us practice. We practiced on our back porch. One day our neighbor leaned out his window in his pajamas and yelled, "Listen, kids, you sound great but give me a break. I work at night. I've got to get some sleep in the daytime." After that we practiced inside. Grandma said it was helping her get better faster than anything.

At last my accordion teacher said we sounded very good. Uncle Sandy said so too. Aunt Ida and Grandma said we were terrific. Mama said she thought anyone would be glad to have us play for them.

It was Leora's mother who gave us our first job.
She asked us to come and play at a party for Leora's
great-grandmother and great-grandfather. It was going
to be a special anniversary for them. It was fifty years
ago on that day they first opened their market on our
corner. Now Leora's mother takes care of the market.
She always plays the radio loud while she works. But
for the party she said there just had to be live music.

All of Leora's aunts and uncles and cousins came to the party. Lots of people from our block came too. Mama and Aunt Ida and Uncle Sandy walked down from our house very slowly with Grandma. It was Grandma's first big day out.

There was a long table in the backyard made from little tables all pushed together. It was covered with so many big dishes of food you could hardly see the tablecloth. But I was too excited to eat anything.

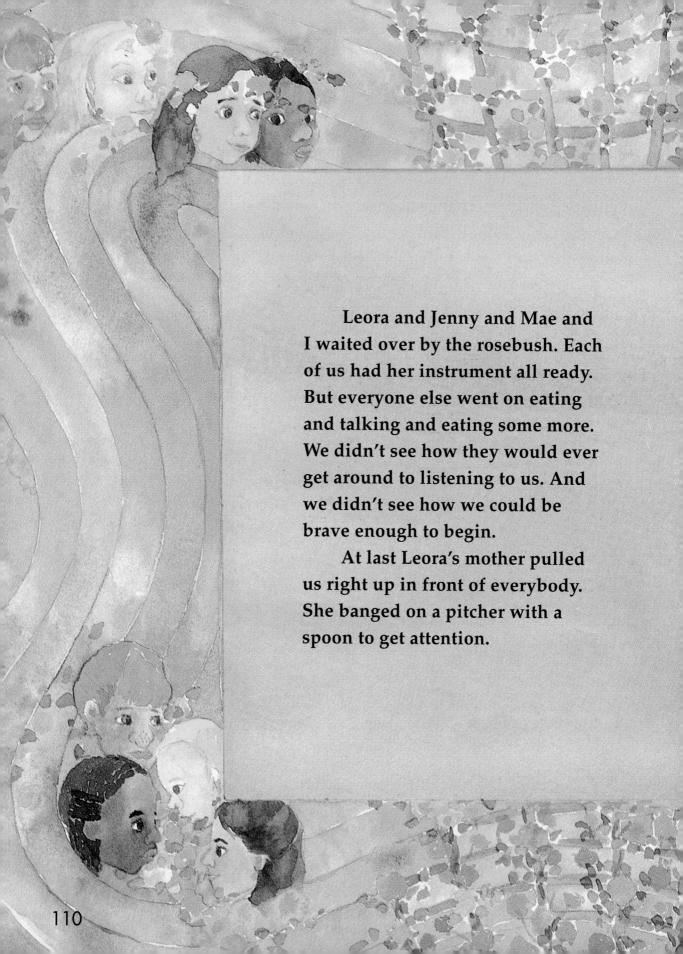

Leora and Jenny and Mae and I waited over by the rosebush. Each of us had her instrument all ready. But everyone else went on eating and talking and eating some more. We didn't see how they would ever get around to listening to us. And we didn't see how we could be brave enough to begin.

At last Leora's mother pulled us right up in front of everybody. She banged on a pitcher with a spoon to get attention.

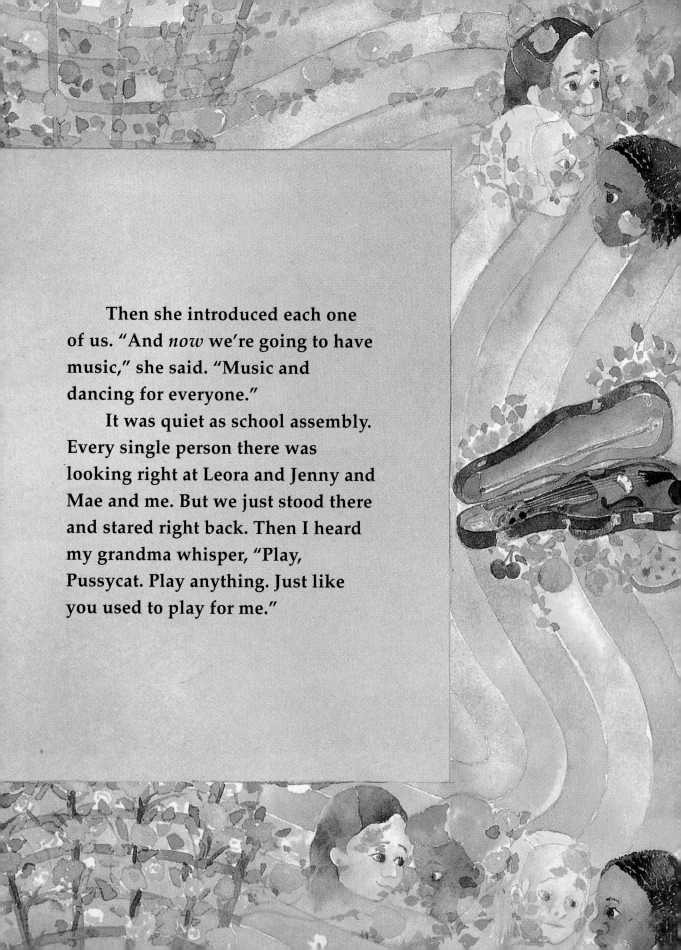

Then she introduced each one of us. "And *now* we're going to have music," she said. "Music and dancing for everyone."

It was quiet as school assembly. Every single person there was looking right at Leora and Jenny and Mae and me. But we just stood there and stared right back. Then I heard my grandma whisper, "Play, Pussycat. Play anything. Just like you used to play for me."

I put my fingers on the keys and buttons of my accordion. Jenny tucked her fiddle under her chin. Mae put her flute to her mouth. Leora held up her drums. After that we played and played. We made mistakes, but we played like a real band. The little lanterns came on. Everyone danced.

Mama and Aunt Ida and Uncle Sandy smiled at us every time they danced by. Grandma kept time nodding her head and tapping with the cane she uses now. Leora and Jenny and Mae and I forgot about being scared. We loved the sound of the Oak Street Band.

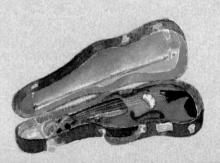

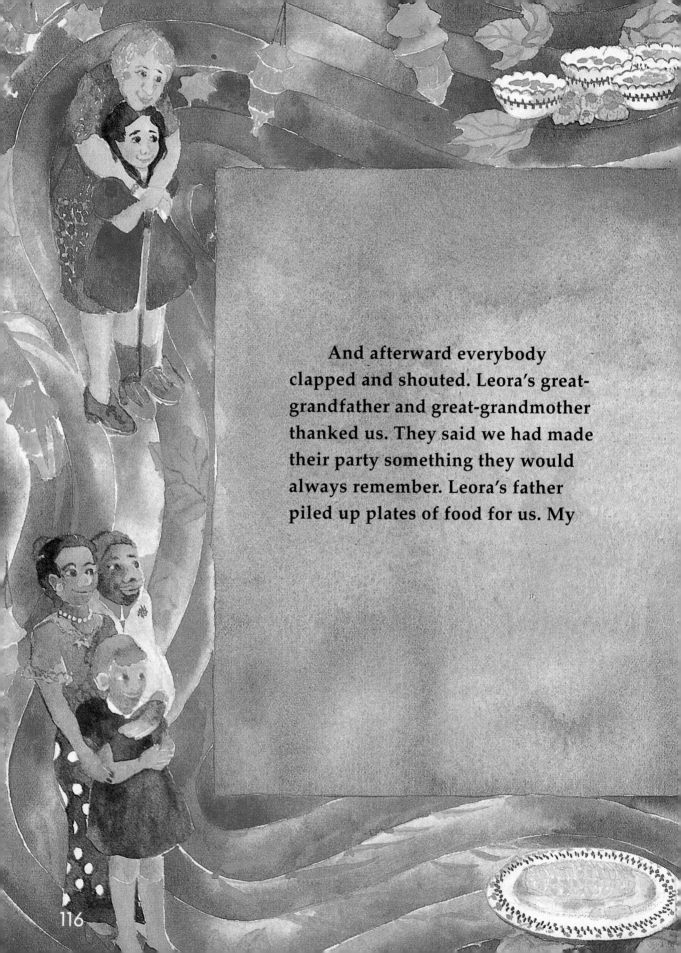

And afterward everybody clapped and shouted. Leora's great-grandfather and great-grandmother thanked us. They said we had made their party something they would always remember. Leora's father piled up plates of food for us. My

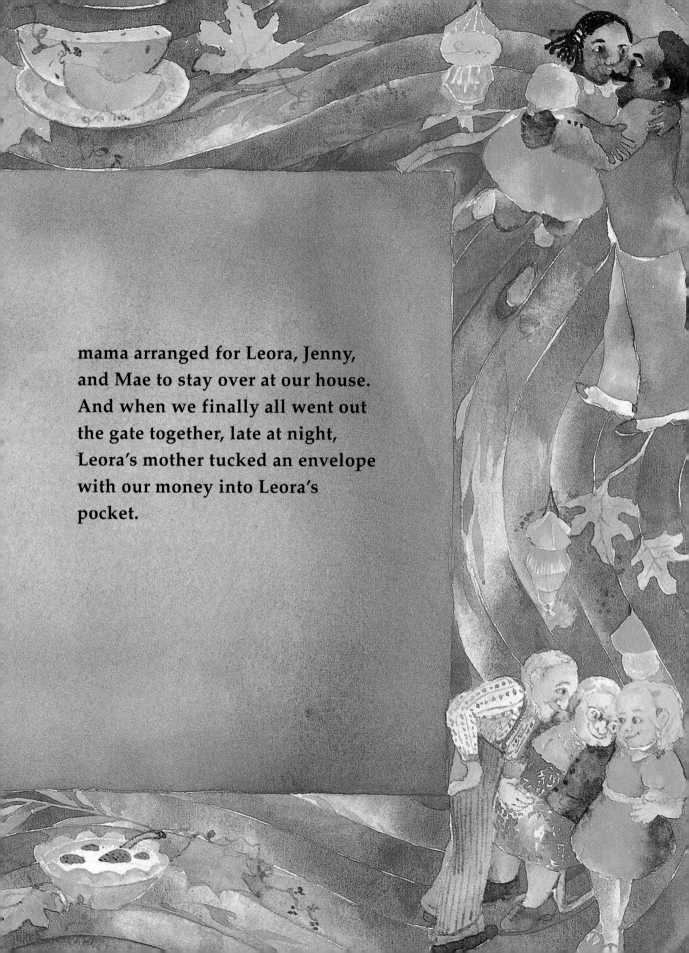

mama arranged for Leora, Jenny,
and Mae to stay over at our house.
And when we finally all went out
the gate together, late at night,
Leora's mother tucked an envelope
with our money into Leora's
pocket.

As soon as we got home, we piled into my bed to divide the money. We made four equal shares. Leora said she was going to save up for a bigger drum. Mae wasn't sure what she would do with her share. Jenny fell asleep before she could tell us. But I couldn't even lie down until I climbed up and put mine right into our big jar on the shelf near our chair.

Think about the part of the story that meant the most to you. Use your own words to retell your favorite part of the story to a friend.

Rosa, the main character, uses her music to help her family. What could you imagine doing to help other people who are having troubles?

WRITE In this story, Rosa worries about her sick grandma and the empty money jar. Write your opinions about happy stories and sad stories and which you'd rather read. Tell about different stories you remember or tell one from your own life that would make a good book.

WORDS FROM THE AUTHOR AND ILLUSTRATOR

Dear Readers and Lookers,

I'm glad you've had a chance to read my story in this collection. The complete story is printed here just as I wrote it. But it wasn't possible to put in all the pictures and borders and backgrounds.

I'd like you to see my whole book in a library or bookstore sometime because I planned *Music, Music for Everyone* from the very front cover to the back cover. I painted all the borders and the watercolored backgrounds. I even picked out the kind of alphabet letters to use from the hundreds of kinds that the printing company has.

First I wrote the story. It took about a month till I got it just right. After that I made a sample book of the right size and glued in copies of the paragraphs and sketches. I tried different arrangements for the pages. When I made the paintings I had to imagine how everyone should look and all the rooms and all the food. Everything. That's the most exciting part for me.

While I worked I had the radio on. I listened to all kinds of music, and I think that music is in the colors and wave shapes of the borders now for everyone to see.

Vera B Williams

AWARD-WINNING
AUTHOR

Listen to This!

As you read these selections, you learned about musical instruments and about how music can make people happy. Can you think of something other than music that can make you happy?

WRITER'S WORKSHOP

Think about your favorite music. Then write a paragraph that describes how that music sounds and how it makes you feel.

Writer's Choice:

You might decide to write about an instrument you would like to play. Or you might invent an instrument and write a description of it. Plan what you would like to write and how you will share it.

CONNECTIONS

Multicultural Connection

Planting Trees in Kenya

For Wangari Maathai [wan•gar´ē mə•tī´], being special has meant working to save the environment of her native land, the East African country of Kenya. In 1977 she founded the Green Belt Movement to plant trees and end *deforestation*—the clearing of forests—in Kenya. For years Kenyans had been cutting down trees to use for firewood and to clear space to plant crops. The land was turning into desert.

Under Maathai's direction, the Green Belt Movement, which is made up mainly of women, has planted ten million trees in Kenya. Maathai has won praise and awards around the world, and the Green Belt idea has spread to a dozen African nations.

Find out what people are doing in your area to save the environment. Share your findings and ideas with your classmates.

Wangari Maathai

People planting trees for the Green Belt Movement

Science/Social Studies Connection

Green Solutions

With a partner, find out about an environmental problem in the world and what's being done about it. Organize your findings on a chart and give a report to your classmates.

Social Studies Connection

Making a Difference

Find out more about Wangari Maathai or another person, such as Mother Teresa or Dr. Pedro José Greer, who has worked to make the world a better place. Write a short report on that person.

Mother Teresa

UNIT TWO

2

Friendships

We're not a bit the same and yet,
We're closer than most people get.

Jean Little

Some friends you see every day, and some friends you may never meet. But how can someone you have never met be a friend? In a way, Antonia Novello was a friend to everyone in the United States, because she was the doctor in charge of our nation's public health program. In what other ways can someone be a friend? Think about this question as you read the next selections.

THEMES

BOOKSHELF

RAMONA QUIMBY, AGE 8
by Beverly Cleary
Ramona Quimby is having a little trouble adjusting to third grade. She wants to be a good student and a help to her family, but sometimes just being Ramona is hard enough.
Newbery Honor Book
Harcourt Brace Library Book

TY'S ONE-MAN BAND
by Mildred Pitts Walter
This original American folktale, created by the author, tells about a peg-legged man named Andro who entertains others as a one-man band. One summer he brings joy to Ty's town through the music he makes.
Award-Winning Author
Harcourt Brace Library Book

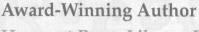

ELAINE, MARY LEWIS, AND THE FROGS

by Heidi Chang

Elaine Chow is very unhappy after moving to a small town in Iowa, until she shares a new friendship and a science project with Mary Lewis, a girl very interested in frogs. Elaine's father teaches them both something about his hobby, which helps them with their project and becomes a symbol of their friendship.

MISTER KING

by Raija Siekkinen

A lonely king who has no subjects is paid a visit by a very unusual cat. The cat brings about many surprises, and the king's life changes in several ways.
Award-Winning Author

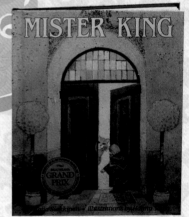

JULIAN'S GLORIOUS SUMMER

by Ann Cameron

Julian is afraid of bicycles, but he has trouble showing his fear to his friend Gloria, who can ride a bike with no hands. Julian goes to amazing lengths to keep bicycles out of his life.
ALA Notable Book

THEME

School Days

While growing up, people often have some funny experiences mixed in with their everyday school activities. You are going to read about a funny character and about the author who created her—Beverly Cleary.

CONTENTS

RAMONA'S Neighborhood

Beverly Cleary was born, attended school, and grew up in Oregon. This walking map of the northeast section of Portland, Oregon, identifies landmarks from some of her books. The places shown on the map were suggested by people who read books in the Henry and Ramona series and searched for clues in them that referred to Portland landmarks. When they found clues, they described what happened there. Even though Beverly Cleary's characters are fictional, Ramona's neighborhood is a real place.

MAP KEY

1 Henry, Beezus, and Ramona live on **Klickitat Street** (*Henry and Ribsy*).

2 Ramona wrote all over *Big Steve*, the book Beezus borrowed from the "Glenwood Library," otherwise known as the **Hollywood Branch of the Multnomah County Library** (*Beezus and Ramona*).

3 **Laurelhurst School,** where Ramona started the third grade at the "Cedarhurst Elementary School" (*Ramona and Her Father*).

4 Ramona got her bridesmaid's dress for Aunt Bea's wedding at **Lloyd Center** (*Ramona Forever*).

5 Ramona and her new boots were stuck in the mud in front of **Kienow's Supermarket** (*Ramona the Pest*).

130

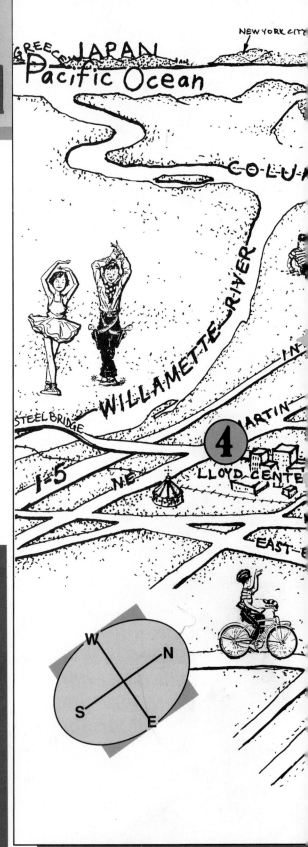

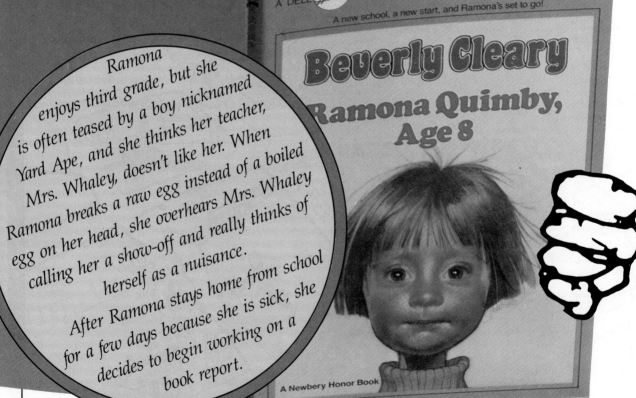

Ramona

enjoys third grade, but she is often teased by a boy nicknamed Yard Ape, and she thinks her teacher, Mrs. Whaley, doesn't like her. When Ramona breaks a raw egg instead of a boiled egg on her head, she overhears Mrs. Whaley calling her a show-off and really thinks of herself as a nuisance.

After Ramona stays home from school for a few days because she is sick, she decides to begin working on a book report.

47350-0 • U.S. $3.25
CAN. $4.50

A DELL YEARLING BOOK

A new school, a new start, and Ramona's set to go!

Beverly Cleary

Ramona Quimby, Age 8

A Newbery Honor Book

Ramona Quimby, AGE 8

by **Beverly Cleary**

illustrated by **Alan Tiegreen**

The book, *The Left-Behind Cat,* which Mrs. Whaley had sent home for Ramona to read for her report, was divided into chapters but used babyish words. The story was about a cat that was left behind when a family moved away and about its adventures with a dog, another cat, and some children before it finally found a home with a nice old couple who gave it a saucer of cream and named it Lefty because its left paw was white and because it had been left behind. Medium-boring, thought Ramona, good enough to pass the time on the bus, but not good enough to read during Sustained Silent Reading. Besides, cream cost too much to give to a cat. The most the old people would give a cat was half-and-half, she thought. Ramona required accuracy from books as well as from people.

NEWBERY HONOR

ALA NOTABLE BOOK

CHILDREN'S CHOICE

"Daddy, how do you sell something?" Ramona interrupted her father, who was studying, even though she knew she should not. However, her need for an answer was urgent.

Mr. Quimby did not look up from his book. "You ought to know. You see enough commercials on television."

Ramona considered his answer. She had always looked upon commercials as entertainment, but now she thought about some of her favorites—the cats that danced back and forth, the dog that pushed away brand-X dog food with his paw, the man who ate a pizza, got indigestion, and groaned that he couldn't believe he ate the *whole* thing, the six horses that pulled the Wells Fargo bank's stagecoach across deserts and over mountains.

"Do you mean I should do a book report like a T.V. commercial?" Ramona asked.

"Why not?" Mr. Quimby answered in an absent-minded way.

"I don't want my teacher to say I'm a nuisance," said Ramona, needing assurance from a grown-up.

This time Mr. Quimby lifted his eyes from his book. "Look," he said, "she told you to pretend you're selling the book, so sell it. What better way than a T.V. commercial? You aren't being a nuisance if you do what your teacher asks." He looked at Ramona a moment and said, "Why do you worry she'd think you're a nuisance?"

Ramona stared at the carpet, wiggled her toes inside her shoes, and finally said, "I squeaked my shoes the first day of school."

"That's not being much of a nuisance," said Mr. Quimby.

"And when I got egg in my hair, Mrs. Whaley said I was a nuisance," confessed Ramona, "and then I threw up in school."

"But you didn't do those things on purpose," her father pointed out. "Now run along. I have studying to do."

Ramona thought this answer over and decided that since her parents agreed, they must be right. Well, Mrs. Whaley could just go jump in a lake, even though her teacher had written, without wasting words, that she missed her. Ramona was going to give her book report any way she wanted. So there, Mrs. Whaley.

Ramona went to her room and looked at her table, which the family called "Ramona's studio," because it was a clutter of crayons, different kinds of paper, Scotch tape, bits of yarn, and odds and ends that Ramona used for amusing herself. Then Ramona thought a moment, and suddenly, filled with inspiration, she went to work. She knew exactly what she wanted to do and set about doing it. She worked with paper, crayons, Scotch tape, and rubber bands. She worked so hard and with such pleasure that her cheeks grew pink. Nothing in the whole world felt as good as being able to make something from a sudden idea.

Finally, with a big sigh of relief, Ramona leaned back in her chair to admire her work: three cat masks with holes for eyes and mouths, masks that could be worn by hooking rubber bands over ears. But Ramona did not stop there. With pencil and paper, she began to write out what she would say. She was so full of ideas that she printed rather than waste time in cursive writing. Next she phoned Sara and Janet, keeping her voice low and trying not to giggle so she wouldn't disturb her father any more than necessary, and explained her plan to them. Both her friends giggled and agreed to take part in the book report. Ramona spent the rest of the evening memorizing what she was going to say.

The next morning on the bus and at school, no one even mentioned Ramona's throwing up. She had braced herself for some remark from Yard Ape, but all he said was, "Hi, Superfoot." When school started, Ramona slipped cat masks to Sara and Janet, handed her written excuse for her absence to Mrs. Whaley, and waited, fanning away escaped fruit flies, for book reports to begin.

After arithmetic, Mrs. Whaley called on several people to come to the front of the room to pretend they were selling books to the class. Most of the reports began, "This is a book about . . ." and many, as Beezus had predicted, ended with ". . . if you want to find out what happens next, read the book."

Then Mrs. Whaley said, "We have time for one more report before lunch. Who wants to be next?"

Ramona waved her hand, and Mrs. Whaley nodded.

Ramona beckoned to Sara and Janet, who giggled in an embarrassed way but joined Ramona, standing behind her and off to one side. All three girls slipped on their cat masks and giggled again. Ramona took a deep breath as Sara and Janet began to chant, "*Meow,* meow, meow, meow. *Meow,* meow, meow, meow," and danced back and forth like the cats they had seen in the cat-food commercial on television.

"*Left-Behind Cat* gives kids something to smile about," said Ramona in a loud clear voice, while her chorus meowed softly behind her. She wasn't sure that what she said was exactly true, but neither were the commercials that showed cats eating dry cat food without making any noise. "Kids who have tried *Left-Behind Cat* are all smiles, smiles, smiles. *Left-Behind Cat* is the book kids ask for by name. Kids can read it every day and thrive on it. The happiest kids read *Left-Behind Cat. Left-Behind Cat* contains cats, dogs, people—" Here Ramona caught sight of Yard Ape leaning back in his seat, grinning in the way that always flustered her. She could not help interrupting herself with a giggle, and after suppressing it she tried not to look at Yard Ape and to take up where she had left off. ". . . cats, dogs, people—" The giggle came back, and Ramona was lost. She could not remember what came next. ". . . cats, dogs, people," she repeated, trying to start and failing.

Mrs. Whaley and the class waited. Yard Ape grinned. Ramona's loyal chorus meowed and danced. This performance could not go on all morning. Ramona had to say something, anything to end the waiting, the meowing, her book report. She tried desperately to recall a cat-food commercial, any cat-food commercial, and could not. All she could remember was the man on

television who ate the pizza, and so she blurted out the only sentence she could think of, "I can't believe I read the *whole* thing!"

Mrs. Whaley's laugh rang out above the laughter of the class. Ramona felt her face turn red behind her mask, and her ears, visible to the class, turned red as well.

"Thank you, Ramona," said Mrs. Whaley. "That was most entertaining. Class, you are excused for lunch."

Ramona felt brave behind her cat mask. "Mrs. Whaley," she said, as the class pushed back chairs and gathered up lunch boxes, "that wasn't the way my report was supposed to end."

"Did you like the book?" asked Mrs. Whaley.

"Not really," confessed Ramona.

"Then I think it was a good way to end your report," said the teacher. "Asking the class to sell books they really don't like isn't fair, now that I stop to think about it. I was only trying to make book reports a little livelier."

Encouraged by this confession and still safe behind her mask, Ramona had the boldness to speak up. "Mrs. Whaley," she said with her heart pounding, "you told Mrs. Larson that I'm a nuisance, and I don't think I am."

Mrs. Whaley looked astonished. "When did I say that?"

"The day I got egg in my hair," said Ramona. "You called me a show-off and said I was a nuisance."

Mrs. Whaley frowned, thinking. "Why, Ramona, I can recall saying something about my little show-off, but I meant it affectionately, and I'm sure I never called you a nuisance."

"Yes, you did," insisted Ramona. "You said I was a show-off, and then you said, 'What a nuisance.'" Ramona could never forget those exact words.

Mrs. Whaley, who had looked worried, smiled in relief. "Oh, Ramona, you misunderstood," she said. "I meant that trying to wash egg out of your hair was a nuisance for Mrs. Larson. I didn't mean that you personally were a nuisance."

Ramona felt a little better, enough to come out from under her mask to say, "I wasn't showing off. I was just trying to crack an egg on my head like everyone else."

Mrs. Whaley's smile was mischievous. "Tell me, Ramona," she said, "don't you ever try to show off?"

Ramona was embarrassed. "Well . . . maybe . . . sometimes, a little," she admitted. Then she added positively, "But I wasn't showing off that day. How could I be showing off when I was doing what everyone else was doing?"

"You've convinced me," said Mrs. Whaley with a big smile. "Now run along and eat your lunch."

Ramona snatched up her lunch box and went jumping down the stairs to the cafeteria. She laughed to herself because she knew exactly what all the boys and girls from her class would say when they finished their lunches. She knew because she planned to say it herself. "I can't believe I ate the *whole* thing!"

If you were Mrs. Whaley, what grade would you give Ramona on her book report? Explain why.

Ramona doesn't remove her mask when she talks to Mrs. Whaley after the commercial. Why do you think she leaves the mask on?

"Ramona is a show-off." Explain why you agree or disagree with the statement.

WRITE   If you had to present a book report as an advertisement, what kind of advertisement would you use? Choose a book you've enjoyed reading, and write the advertisement you would use for it.

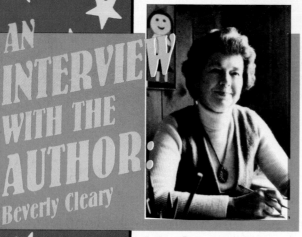

Writer Ilene Cooper spoke with Beverly Cleary to find out how she creates the characters in her books. This interview tells where Ms. Cleary gets the ideas for her characters. It also tells how she became interested in reading and writing.

MS. COOPER: Ramona is so funny, and she comes up with all kinds of interesting ideas, such as the way she did her book report. Were you at all like Ramona when you were a child?

MS. CLEARY: I think I was like Ramona until I started school. I lived on a farm where I was wild and free and could use my imagination. I was allowed to do almost anything I wanted to do as long as it was safe. When I began school, I became much more like Ellen Tebbits, another character.

MS. COOPER: What did you like to read when you were a third and fourth grader?

MS. CLEARY: Well, I read the complete fairy tale section of our branch library. I did have a couple of favorite books when I was in the third and fourth grades—one favorite, but it's out of print now.

MS. COOPER: Did you always like to read?

MS. CLEARY: Oh, no.

MS. COOPER: But you made the change from somebody who didn't like to read to a reader—a real reader.

MS. CLEARY: Yes, in the third grade.

MS. COOPER: What happened then?

MS. CLEARY: The right book. It was *The Dutch Twins* by

Lucy Fitch Perkins. I started to look at the pictures
because I was bored, and I discovered that I was reading
it and enjoying it!

MS. COOPER: Did you write at all when you were that age?

MS. CLEARY: No.

MS. COOPER: You just did school writing?

MS. CLEARY: Just school assignments. But
compositions were always my favorite assignments.

MS. COOPER: What advice would you give to young
people who want to write?

MS. CLEARY: Writing doesn't have to be a story. Why not
write a page of dialogue, such as a quarrel between a
brother and sister? Be original and don't copy. Don't use
characters from other people's books or television
shows. Look around you and find your own
characters. Good writing is original and comes from
within the writer.

MS. COOPER: What do you think about keeping a diary,
or notebook?

MS. CLEARY: I think keeping a diary is useful.

MS. COOPER: What do you think is the hardest thing
about writing, and what do you think is the
easiest thing about writing?

MS. CLEARY: The hardest thing about writing is
pushing through to the end of the story. The
easiest thing is revising. I think all writers
do some revising. That's when I
cross out a lot and reduce a page
to one paragraph. It's necessary
because in my first draft I tend to put in

AWARD-WINNING
AUTHOR

extra material as it comes to mind. And then when I finish I realize that some of it wasn't needed.

MS. COOPER: When you start a book, do you know how it's going to end?

MS. CLEARY: No I don't, and I don't always write stories in order. In *Ramona and Her Father,* I wrote the last chapter first. I begin with the characters and something they would do and just let the story work itself out.

MS. COOPER: That's interesting. You start in the middle and maybe one day you feel like writing about what happened before the incident, and then the next day . . .

MS. CLEARY: I write everything that's vivid to me. And it usually all fits together.

MS. COOPER: Some of the vivid incidents—for example, Ramona breaking the egg over her head—did those things really happen, or did you just make them up?

MS. CLEARY: Well, both. I happened to hear about the egg incident when a group of teachers were talking. Sometimes I write about things that happened in my own childhood, but I change them. Sometimes I want to write about something, and it won't fit into the story. I wanted to write about the time my cat ate my jack-o'-lantern. And it took me about 20 years before that would work into a story.

MS. COOPER: So sometimes you just put an idea into the back of your mind and save it?

MS. CLEARY: Yes, I've had characters wandering about in the back of my mind who will not come into books.

MS. COOPER: They're just waiting for their own stories.

MS. CLEARY: Yes.

School Days

In this theme you read about the school experiences of two girls—Ramona Quimby, a fictional character, and Beverly Cleary, an author. How is the author like the character she created? How is she different?

WRITER'S WORKSHOP

Ramona did a book report on a story she did not especially like. Choose a story you did not especially like and write a new ending for it.

Writer's Choice:

Writing does not always have to be a story. Write an imaginary conversation between two people. Or write a commercial for a book. Plan what you will write and how you will share it.

T H E M E

Caring and Sharing

Giving of yourself—your time and your friendship—is a special way of sharing with others. The following stories and poem tell about some special ways that people show they care.

C O N T E N T S

149

THROUGH GRANDPA'S EYES

by Patricia MacLachlan

illustrated by Greg Shed

Of all the houses that I know,
I like my grandpa's best. My friend
Peter has a new glass house with pebble-path
gardens that go nowhere. And Maggie lives next door
in an old wooden house with rooms behind rooms, all
with carved doors and brass doorknobs. They are fine
houses. But Grandpa's house is my favorite. Because I
see it through Grandpa's eyes.

Grandpa is blind. He doesn't see the house the way I do. He has his own way of seeing.

In the morning, the sun pushes through the curtains into my eyes. I burrow down into the covers to get away, but the light follows me. I give up, throw back the covers, and run to Grandpa's room.

The sun wakes Grandpa differently from the way it wakes me. He says it touches him, *warming* him awake. When I peek around the door, Grandpa is already up and doing his morning exercises. Bending and stretching by the bed. He stops and smiles because he hears me.

"Good morning, John."

"Where's Nana?" I ask him.

"Don't you know?" he says, bending and stretching. "Close your eyes, John, and look through my eyes."

I close my eyes. Down below, I hear the banging of pots and the sound of water running that I didn't hear before.

"Nana is in the kitchen, making breakfast," I say.

When I open my eyes again, I can see Grandpa nodding at me. He is tall with dark gray hair. And his eyes are sharp blue even though they are not sharp seeing.

I exercise with Grandpa. Up and down. Then I try to exercise with my eyes closed.

"One, two," says Grandpa, "three, four."

"Wait!" I cry. I am still on one, two when Grandpa is on three, four.

I fall sideways. Three times. Grandpa laughs as he hears my thumps on the carpet.

"Breakfast!" calls Nana from downstairs.

"I smell eggs frying," says Grandpa. He bends his head close to mine. "And buttered toast."

The wooden banister on the stairway has been worn smooth from Grandpa running his fingers up and down. I walk behind him, my fingers following Grandpa's smooth path.

We go into the kitchen.

"I smell flowers," says Grandpa.

"What flowers?" I ask.

He smiles. He loves guessing games.

"Not violets, John, not peonies . . ."

"Carnations!" I cry. *I* love guessing games.

"Silly." Grandpa laughs. "Marigolds. Right, Nana?"

Nana laughs, too.

"That's too easy," she says, putting two plates of food in front of us.

"It's not too easy," I protest. "How can Grandpa tell? All the smells mix together in the air."

"Close your eyes, John," says Nana. "Tell me what breakfast is."

"I smell the eggs. I smell the toast," I say, my eyes closed. "And something else. The something else doesn't smell good."

"*That* something else," says Nana smiling, "is the marigolds."

When he eats, Grandpa's plate of food is a clock.

"Two eggs at nine o'clock and toast at two o'clock," says Nana to Grandpa. "And a dollop of jam."

"A dollop of jam," I tell Grandpa, "at six o'clock."

I make my plate of food a clock, too, and eat through Grandpa's eyes.

After breakfast, I follow Grandpa's path through the dining room to the living room, to the window that he opens to feel the weather outside, to the table where he finds his pipe, and to his cello in the corner.

"Will you play with me, John?" he asks.

He tunes our cellos without looking. I play with a music stand and music before me. I know all about sharps and flats. I see them on the music. But Grandpa plays them. They are in his fingers. For a moment I close my eyes and play through Grandpa's eyes. My fingering hand slides up and down the cello neck—toward the pegs for flats, toward the bridge for sharps. But with my eyes closed my bow falls from the strings.

"Listen," says Grandpa. "I'll play a piece I learned when I was your age. It was my favorite."

He plays the tune while I listen. That is the way Grandpa learns new pieces. By listening.

"Now," says Grandpa. "Let's do it together."

"That's fine," says Grandpa as we play. "But C sharp, John," he calls to me. "C sharp!"

Later, Nana brings out her clay to sculpt my Grandpa's head.

"Sit still," she grumbles.

"I won't," he says, imitating her grumbly voice, making us laugh.

While she works, Grandpa takes out his piece of wood. He holds it when he's thinking. His fingers move back and forth across the wood, making smooth paths like the ones on the stair banister.

"Can I have a piece of thinking wood, too?" I ask.

Grandpa reaches in his shirt pocket and tosses a small bit of wood in my direction. I catch it. It is smooth with no splinters.

"The river is up," says Nana.

Grandpa nods a short nod. "It rained again last night. Did you hear the gurgling in the rain gutter?"

As they talk, my fingers begin a river on my thinking wood. The wood will winter in my pocket so when I am not at Grandpa's house I can still think about Nana, Grandpa, and the river.

When Nana is finished working, Grandpa runs his hand over the sculpture, his fingers soft and quick like butterflies.

"It looks like me," he says, surprised.

My eyes have already told me that it looks like Grandpa. But he shows me how to feel his face with my three middle fingers, and then the clay face.

"Pretend your fingers are water," he tells me.

My waterfall fingers flow down his clay head, filling in the spaces beneath the eyes like little pools before they flow down over the cheeks. It does feel like Grandpa. This time my fingers tell me.

Grandpa and I walk outside, through the front yard and across the field to the river. Grandpa has not been blind forever. He remembers in his mind the gleam of the sun on the river, the Queen Anne's lace in the meadow, and every dahlia in his garden. But he gently takes my elbow as we walk so that I can help show him the path.

"I feel a south wind," says Grandpa.

I can tell which way the wind is blowing because I see the way the tops of the trees lean. Grandpa tells by the feel of the meadow grasses and by the way his hair blows against his face.

When we come to the riverbank, I see that Nana was right. The water is high and has cut in by the willow tree. It flows around and among the roots of the tree, making paths. Paths like Grandpa's on the stair banister and on the thinking wood. I see a blackbird with a red patch on its wing sitting on a cattail. Without thinking, I point my finger.

"What is that bird, Grandpa?" I ask excitedly.

"*Conk-a-ree*," the bird calls to us.

"A red-winged blackbird," says Grandpa promptly.

He can't see my finger pointing. But he hears the song of the bird.

"And somewhere behind the blackbird," he says, listening, "a song sparrow."

I hear a scratchy song, and I look and look until I see the earth-colored bird that Grandpa knows is here.

Nana calls from the front porch of the house.

"Nana's made hot bread for lunch," he tells me happily. "And spice tea." Spice tea is his favorite.

I close my eyes, but all I can smell is the wet earth by the river.

As we walk back to the house, Grandpa stops suddenly. He bends his head to one side, listening. He points his finger upward.

"Honkers," he whispers.

I look up and see a flock of geese, high in the clouds, flying in a *V.*

"Canada geese," I tell him.

"Honkers," he insists. And we both laugh.

We walk up the path again and to the yard where Nana is painting the porch chairs. Grandpa smells the paint.

"What color, Nana?" he asks. "I cannot smell the color."

"Blue," I tell him, smiling. "Blue like the sky."

"Blue like the color of Grandpa's eyes," Nana says.

When he was younger, before I can remember, before he was blind, Grandpa did things the way I do. Now, when we drink tea and eat lunch on the porch, Grandpa pours his own cup of tea by putting his finger just inside the rim of the cup to tell him when it is full. He never burns his finger. Afterward, when I wash the dishes, he feels them as he dries them. He even sends some back for me to wash again.

"Next time," says Grandpa, pretending to be cross, "I wash, you dry."

In the afternoon, Grandpa, Nana, and I take our books outside to read under the apple tree. Grandpa reads his book with his fingers, feeling the raised Braille dots that tell him the words.

As he reads, Grandpa laughs out loud.

"Tell us what's funny," says Nana. "Read to us, Papa." And he does.

Nana and I put down our books to listen. A gray squirrel comes down the trunk of the apple tree, tail high, and seems to listen, too. But Grandpa doesn't see him.

After supper, Grandpa turns on the television. I watch, but Grandpa listens, and the music and the words tell him when something is dangerous or funny, happy or sad.

Somehow, Grandpa knows when it is dark, and he takes me upstairs and tucks me into bed. He bends down to kiss me, his hands feeling my head.

"You need a haircut, John," he says.

Before Grandpa leaves, he pulls the light chain above my bed to turn out the light. But, by mistake, he's turned it on instead. I lie for a moment after he's gone, smiling, before I get up to turn off the light.

Then, when it is dark for me the way it is dark for Grandpa, I hear the night noises that Grandpa hears. The house creaking, the birds singing their last songs of the day, the wind rustling the tree outside my window.

Then, all of a sudden, I hear the sounds of geese overhead. They fly low over the house.

"Grandpa," I call softly, hoping he's heard them too.

"Honkers," he calls back.

"Go to sleep, John," says Nana.

Grandpa says her voice smiles to him. I test it.

"What?" I call to her.

"I said go to sleep," she answers.

She says it sternly. But Grandpa is right. Her voice smiles to me. I know. Because I'm looking through Grandpa's eyes.

What did you learn about the way John sees "through Grandpa's eyes"?

What makes John's relationship with his grandfather special?

How are Grandpa's fingers like John's eyes?

WRITE Write a description of an object for a friend. Use words that will help him or her "see" the object without actually looking at it.

Writers

by Jean Little
illustrated by Roberta Ludlow

Emily writes of poetic things
Like crocuses and hummingbirds' wings,
But I think people beat hummingbirds every time.

Emily likes to write of snow
And dawn and candlelight aglow,
But I'd rather write about me and Emily and stuff like that.

The funny thing is, I delight
To read what Emily likes to write,
And Emily says she thinks my poems are okay too.

Also, sometimes, we switch with each other.
Emily writes of a fight with her mother.
I tell about walking alone by the river,
   —how still and golden it was.

I know what Emily means, you see,
And, often, Emily's halfway me. . . .
Oh, there's just no way to make anybody else understand.

We're not a bit the same and yet,
We're closer than most people get.
There's no one word for it. We just care about each other
   the way we are supposed to.

So I can look through Emily's eyes
And she through mine. It's no surprise,
When you come right down to it, that we're friends.

AWARD-WINNING
AUTHOR

A Gift for Tía Rosa

by Karen T. Taha

"AROUND, OVER, THROUGH, AND PULL. Around, over, through, and pull," Carmela repeated as she knitted. A rainbow of red, orange, and gold wool stretched almost to her feet. Now and then she stopped and listened for her father's car. He mustn't see what she was knitting!

The rumble of a motor made her drop the needles and run to the window. In the gray November shadows, she saw a battered brown station wagon turn into the garage next door.

illustrated by Laura Kelly

170

"Mamá, she's home! Tía Rosa is home!" Carmela called. Carmela's mother hurried out of the bedroom. She put her arm around Carmela. They watched as lights flickered on in the windows, bringing the neat white house back to life.

"I know you want to see Tía Rosa, Carmela," said her mother, "but she and Tío Juan have had a long trip. Tía Rosa must be very tired after two weeks in the hospital."

"But can I call her, Mamá?" asked Carmela. "The scarf for Papá is almost done. She promised to help me fringe it when she came home."

"No, Carmela. Not now," her mother replied firmly. "Tía Rosa needs to rest." She smoothed back Carmela's thick black hair from her face.

Carmela tossed her head. "But Mamá . . . !"

"No, Carmela!"

Carmela knew there was no use arguing. But it wasn't fair. Tomorrow she would have to go to school. She couldn't see Tía Rosa until the afternoon. Her mother just didn't understand.

Frowning, Carmela plopped back on the sofa and picked up the silver knitting needles. At least she would finish more of the scarf before Tía Rosa saw it tomorrow. She bent over her knitting and began once more. "Around, over, through, and pull." The phone rang in the kitchen.

"I'll get it!" Carmela shouted, bounding into the hall. "Hello?" Her dark eyes sparkled. "Tía Rosa! You must see Papá's scarf. It's almost finished . . . You did? For me? Okay, I'll be right there!"

The phone clattered as Carmela hung up. "Mamá! Tía Rosa wants to see the scarf. She even brought me a surprise!"

Carmela's mother smiled and shook her head. "Tía Rosa is unbelievable."

Carmela stuffed the bright wool into her school bag. "I'm going to make Tía Rosa a surprise after I finish Papá's scarf!" she called as she ran out.

She ran across the yard to Tía Rosa's front door. The door swung open, and there was Tío Juan. He looked taller and thinner than she remembered, and his eyes looked sad.

Tío Juan was as tall as Tía Rosa was short, Carmela thought. He was as thin as Tía Rosa was plump. And he was as good at listening as Tía Rosa was at talking.

"*Hola*, Carmelita," he said, bending to kiss her cheek. He led her down the hall. "Tía Rosa is sitting up in bed. She's tired, but she wanted to see her favorite neighbor."

Tía Rosa in bed! In all her eight years Carmela had never seen Tía Rosa sick. She held her breath and peeked into the bedroom. Tía Rosa's round face crinkled into a smile when she saw Carmela.

"Carmelita, come give me a hug!"

Hugging Tía Rosa always made Carmela feel safe and warm. Tía Rosa was like a soft pillow that smelled of soap and bath powder and sometimes of sweet tamales. Now there was another smell, a dentist office smell, Carmela decided.

"Carmelita, I've missed you!" said Tía Rosa. "Let's look at what you have knitted."

Carmela handed her the scarf. Tía Rosa smiled. "Your papá will be proud to wear it," she said. "Tomorrow I'll show you how to fringe it, and I will start on the pink baby blanket for my granddaughter!"

Carmela laughed. "How do you know that Pepe's wife will have a girl?" she asked. Pepe was the oldest of Tía Rosa's six sons.

"Because," answered Tía Rosa with a grin, "anyone who has six sons and no daughters, deserves a granddaughter!"

"But Tía Rosa, what if the baby is a boy? Won't you love him just the same?"

"Of course," laughed Tía Rosa.

Carmela knew Tía Rosa would love the baby, boy or girl, but she crossed her fingers and wished for a girl, too.

"Now for the surprise!" said Tía Rosa. She handed Carmela a small white box. "Go on now. See what's inside."

Carmela opened the box carefully. A snowy ball of cotton lay inside. As she pulled at the cotton, her fingers touched something hard and very small. She heard the "clish" of a chain as she lifted the surprise from under the cotton. In her hand Carmela held a tiny silver rose on a fine chain.

"Oh, Tía Rosa. It's beautiful!" exclaimed Carmela.

"The rose is so you'll remember your old Tía Rosa," she said.

"How could I forget you, Tía Rosa?" asked Carmela. "You're right here!"

Before she went home, Carmela put the rose around her neck. She promised to return the next day after school.

Carmela returned the next day, and the next, and every day for a whole week. Tía Rosa stayed in her room, and Tío Juan moved a chair by the bed for Carmela. Together the two friends worked on their surprise gifts.

"Why does Tía Rosa stay in bed all the time?" Carmela asked her father at breakfast one day.

Her father looked away for a moment. Then he took Carmela's hands in his. "Tía Rosa is very sick, Carmela. The doctors don't think she can get well," he explained.

"But Papá," said Carmela. "I have been sick lots of times. Remember when Tía Rosa stayed with me when you and Mamá had to go away?"

"Yes," answered her father. "But Tía Rosa . . ."

Carmela didn't listen. "Now I will stay with Tía Rosa until she gets well, too," she said.

Every afternoon Carmela worked on her father's scarf. The fringe was the easiest part. With Tía Rosa's help she would have the scarf finished long before Christmas.

Tía Rosa worked on the pink baby blanket, but the needles didn't fly in her sure brown fingers like they once did. Carmela teased her. "Tía Rosa, are you knitting slowly because you might have to change the pink yarn to blue when the baby is born?"

"No, no," replied Tía Rosa with a grin. "The baby will surely be a girl. We need girls in this family. You're the only one I have!"

Sometimes Tía Rosa fell asleep with her knitting still in her hands. Then Carmela would quietly put the needles and yarn into Tía Rosa's big green knitting bag and tiptoe out of the room.

Carmela liked Saturdays and Sundays best because she could spend more time at Tía Rosa's. Mamá always sent a plate of cookies with her, and Tío Juan made hot chocolate for them.

One Saturday morning when Carmela rang the doorbell, Tío Juan didn't come. Carmela ran to the garage and peeked in the window. The brown station wagon was gone.

She returned home and called Tía Rosa's number. The phone rang and rang. Carmela went down the steps to the basement. Her mother was rubbing stain into the freshly sanded wood of an old desk.

"Tía Rosa isn't home," said Carmela sadly. Her mother looked up from her work.

"I thought I heard a car in the night," said her mother. "Surely Tío Juan would have called us if . . ."

Just then the phone rang upstairs. Carmela heard footsteps creak across the floor as her father walked to answer it.

Moments later the footsteps thumped softly towards the basement door. Carmela's father came slowly down the steps. Carmela shivered when she saw his sad face. He put his arms around Carmela and her mother and hugged them close. "Tía Rosa is gone," he whispered. "She died early this morning."

No, her father's words couldn't be true. Carmela didn't believe it. Tía Rosa would come back. She had always come back before.

"It's not true!" cried Carmela. She broke away from her mother and father and raced up the stairs. She ran out the front door and through the yard to Tía Rosa's house. She pushed the doorbell again and again. She pounded on the silent door until her fists hurt. At last she sank down on the steps.

Later her father came. With a soft hanky he brushed the tears from her cheeks. At last they walked quietly home.

The next days were long and lonely for Carmela. She didn't care that Papá's finished scarf lay hidden in her closet, bright and beautiful. She didn't want to see it. She didn't want to feel the cool, smooth knitting needles in her hands ever again.

The white house next door was busy with people coming and going. Carmela took over food her mother and father cooked, but she quickly returned home. She didn't like to see Tío Juan. Seeing Tío Juan made her miss Tía Rosa even more.

One day Carmela said to her mother, "Tía Rosa died before I could give her anything, Mamá. She baked me cookies and taught me to knit and brought me surprises. I was going to surprise her. Now it's too late."

"Carmela, Tía Rosa didn't want her kindness returned. She wanted it passed on," said her mother. "That way a part of Tía Rosa will never die."

"But I wanted to give something to her!" shouted Carmela. "Just to Tía Rosa. To show her that I loved her!"

"She knew that, Carmela. Every smile and hug and visit told her that you loved her," said her mother. "Now it's Tío Juan who needs our love."

"I know," answered Carmela in a soft voice, "but it's hard, Mamá. It hurts so much without Tía Rosa."

One night Carmela's mother asked Tío Juan to dinner. Carmela met him at the door. This time Carmela did not turn away when she saw his sad eyes. Instead, she hugged him tightly.

For the first time in a week, Tío Juan smiled. "Carmelita, tomorrow you must come next door. I would like you to meet my new granddaughter. Her parents have named her Rosita, little Rose, after her grandmother."

Carmela looked down at her silver rose necklace so Tío Juan would not see the tears in her eyes. Tía Rosa knew the baby would be a girl. Then Carmela remembered the unfinished blanket. "Now I know what I can give!" she said.

After dinner Tío Juan went back to the white house. A few minutes later he returned with Tía Rosa's big knitting bag. Very carefully Carmela pulled out the half-finished blanket and wound the soft pink yarn around the needle.

"Around, over, through, and pull. Around, over, through, and pull." Carmela smiled. At last she had a gift for Tía Rosa.

Would you describe this story as a happy one or a sad one? Give reasons for your choice.

Name some of the ways Carmela and Tía Rosa show that they care for one another.

How does Carmela pass on Tía Rosa's kindness?

WRITE   Think of a perfect gift for someone. Write a paragraph that tells why the gift is perfect.

Caring and Sharing

The selections you have just read are about caring for someone and sharing with that person. How can *you* show someone you care? How can you share part of yourself with that person?

WRITER'S WORKSHOP

Think about something you know how to do, and write a paragraph to tell someone else how to do it. Write each step in order.

Writer's Choice:
You might like to write about a very special gift you gave or were given. Choose what you will write. After you are finished, share your writing.

T H E M E

Learning About Yourself

Spending time with other people can help you learn about yourself. It can also help you learn to do new things. The story, the words from the author, and the poem you are about to read may help you learn new things. Maybe you can share what you learn with a friend.

C O N T E N T S

Justin and the Best Biscuits in the World

by Mildred Pitts Walter

illustrated by Brian Deines

Justin lives in the city and is usually surrounded by women—his mother and his two older sisters. Justin's sisters, Evelyn and Hadiya, often complain that he can't do anything right. He starts to believe he can't do "women's work," and the shame of it brings him to tears when his grandfather visits his family. When Justin stays on his grandpa's ranch for a while, he begins to look at things differently.

CORETTA SCOTT
KING AWARD

189

GRANDPA'S HOUSE SAT about a mile in from the road. Between that road and the house lay a large meadow with a small stream. Everything seemed in order when Justin and Grandpa arrived.

Justin got out and opened the gate to the winding road that led toward the house. The meadow below shimmered in waves of tall green grass. The horses grazed calmly there. Justin was so excited to see them again that he waved his grandpa on. "I'll walk up, Grandpa." He ran down into the meadow.

Pink prairie roses blossomed near the fence. Goldenrod, sweet william, and black-eyed susans added color here and there. Justin waded through the lush green grass.

The horses, drinking at the stream, paid no attention as he raced across the meadow toward them. *Cropper looks so old,* he thought as he came closer. But Black Lightning's coat shone, as beautiful as ever. Justin gave a familiar whistle. The horses lifted their heads and their ears went back, but only Black moved toward him on the run.

Justin reached up and
Black lowered his head.
Justin rubbed him behind
the ear. Softly he said,
"Good boy, Black. I've missed
you. You glad to see me?"

Then Pal nosed in,
wanting to be petted, too.
Cropper didn't bother. Justin wondered if Cropper's
eyesight was fading.

The sun had moved well toward the west. Long
shadows from the rolling hills reached across the plains.
"Want to take me home, boy?" Justin asked Black.

Black lowered his head and pawed with one foot as he
shook his mane. Justin led him to a large rock. From the
rock, Justin straddled Black's back, without a saddle. Black
walked him home.

Grandpa's house stood on a hill surrounded by plains,
near the rolling hills. Over many years, trees standing

close by the house
had grown tall and
strong. The house,
more than a
hundred years old,
was made of logs.
The sun and rain
had turned the
logs on the outside

an iron gray. Flecks of green showed in some of the logs.

When Justin went inside, Grandpa had already changed his clothes. Now he busily measured food for the animals. While Grandpa was away, a neighbor had come to feed the pigs and chickens. The horses took care of themselves, eating and drinking in the meadow. Today the horses would have some oats, too.

"Let's feed the animals first," Grandpa said. "Then we'll cook those fish for dinner. You can clean them when we get back."

Justin sighed deeply. How could he tell Grandpa he didn't know how to clean fish? He was sure to make a mess of it. Worriedly, he helped Grandpa load the truck with the food and water for the chickens and pigs. They put in oats for the horses, too. Then they drove to the chicken yard.

As they rode along the dusty road, Justin remembered Grandpa telling him that long, long ago they had raised hundreds of cattle on Q-T Ranch. Then when Justin's mama was a little girl, they had raised only chickens on the ranch, selling many eggs to people in the cities. Now Grandpa had only a few chickens, three pigs, and three horses.

At the chicken yard, chickens rushed around to get the bright yellow corn that Justin threw to them. They fell over each other, fluttering and clucking. While Justin fed them, Grandpa gathered the eggs.

The pigs lazily dozed in their pens. They had been wallowing in the mud pond nearby. Now cakes of dried mud dotted their bodies. The floor where they slept had mud on it, too. Many flies buzzed around. *My room surely doesn't look like this*, Justin thought.

The pigs ran to the trough when Grandpa came with the pail of grain mixed with water. They grunted and snorted. The smallest one squealed with delight. *He's cute*, Justin thought.

By the time they had fed the horses oats and returned home, it was dark and cooler. Justin was glad it was so late. Maybe now Grandpa would clean the fish so that they could eat sooner. He was hungry.

Grandpa had not changed the plan. He gave Justin

some old newspapers, a small sharp knife, and a bowl with clean water.

"Now," he said, handing Justin the pail that held the fish, "you can clean these."

Justin looked at the slimy fish in the water. How could he tell his grandpa that he didn't want to touch those fish? He still didn't want Grandpa to know that he had never cleaned fish before. Evelyn's words crowded him: *Can't do anything right.* He dropped his shoulders and sighed. "Do I have to, Grandpa?"

"We have to eat, don't we?"

"But—but I don't know how," Justin cried.

"Oh, it's not hard. I'll show you." Grandpa placed a fish on the newspaper. "Be careful now and keep it on this paper. When you're all done, just fold the paper and all the mess is inside."

Justin watched Grandpa scrape the fish upward from the tail toward the head. Little shiny scales came off easily. Then he cut the fish's belly upward from a little vent hole and scraped all the stuff inside onto the paper. "Now see how easy that is. You try," Grandpa said. "Be very careful with the knife." He watched Justin to see if he knew what to do.

Justin scraped the tiny scales off confidently. Then he hesitated. Screwing up his face, he shuddered as he cut, then pulled the insides out. Finally he got the knack of it.

Grandpa, satisfied that Justin would do fine, went into the kitchen to make a fire in the big stove.

Later that evening, Justin felt proud when Grandpa let him put the fish on the table.

After dinner, they sat in the living room near the huge fireplace. Great-Great-Grandma Ward had used that same fireplace to cook her family's meals.

Justin looked at the fireplace, trying to imagine how it must have been then. *How did people cook without a stove?* He knew Grandpa's stove was nothing like his mama's. Once that big iron stove got hot there was no way to turn it off or to low or to simmer. You just set the pots in a cooler place on the back of Grandpa's stove.

"Grandpa, how did your grandma cook bread in this fireplace?" he asked.

"Cooking bread in this fireplace was easy for my grandma. She once had to bake her bread on a hoe."

"But a hoe is for making a garden, Grandpa."

"Yes, I know, and it was that kind of hoe that she used. She chopped cotton with her hoe down in Tennessee. There was no fireplace in the family's little one-room house, so she cooked with a fire outside. She had no nice iron pots and skillets like I have now in the kitchen.

"At night when the family came in from the cotton

fields, Grandma made a simple bread with cornmeal and a little flour. She patted it and dusted it with more flour. Then she put it on the iron hoe and stuck it in the ashes. When it was nice and brown the ashes brushed off easily."

"How did they ever get from Tennessee to Missouri?"

"Justin, I've told you that so many times."

"I know, Grandpa. But I like to hear it. Tell me again."

"As a boy, my grandpa was a slave. Right after slavery my grandpa worked on a ranch in Tennessee. He rode wild mustangs and tamed them to become good riding horses. He cared so much about horses, he became a cowboy.

"He got married and had a family. Still he left home for many weeks, sometimes months, driving thousands of cattle over long trails. Then he heard about the government giving away land in the West through the Homestead Act. You only had to build a house and live in it to keep the land."

"So my great-great-grandpa built this house." Justin stretched out on the floor. He looked around at the walls that were now dark brown from many years of smoke from the fireplace.

"Just the room we're in now," Grandpa said.

197

"I guess every generation of Wards has added something. Now, my daddy, Phillip, added on the kitchen and the room right next to this one that is the dining room.

"I built the bathroom and the rooms upstairs. Once we had a high loft. I guess you'd call it an attic. I made that into those rooms upstairs. So you see, over the years this house has grown and grown. Maybe when you're a man, you'll bring your family here," Grandpa said.

"I don't know. Maybe. But I'd have to have an electric kitchen."

"As I had to have a bathroom with a shower. Guess that's progress," Grandpa said, and laughed.

"Go on, Grandpa. Tell me what it was like when Great-Great-Grandpa first came to Missouri."

"I think it's time for us to go to bed."

"It's not that late," Justin protested.

"For me it is. We'll have to get up early. I'll have to ride fence tomorrow. You know, in winter Q-T Ranch becomes a feeder ranch for other people's cattle. In spring, summer, and early fall cattle roam and graze in the high country. In winter when the heavy frosts come and it's bitter cold, they return to the plains. Many of those cattle feed at Q-T.

I have to have my fences mended before fall so the cattle can't get out."

"Can I ride fence with you?" Justin asked.

"Sure you can. Maybe you'll like riding fence. That's a man's work." Grandpa laughed.

Justin remembered that conversation in his room about women's work, and the tears. He burned with shame. He didn't laugh.

Upstairs, Grandpa gave Justin sheets and a blanket for his bed. "It'll be cool before morning," he told Justin. "You'll need this blanket. Can you make your bed?"

Justin frowned. He hated making his bed. But he looked at Grandpa and said, "I'm no baby." Justin joined Grandpa in laughter.

Grandpa went to his room. When he was all ready for bed, he came and found Justin still struggling to make his bed. Those sheets had to be made nice and smooth to impress Grandpa, Justin thought, but it wasn't easy.

Grandpa watched. "Want to see how a man makes a bed?" Grandpa asked.

Justin didn't answer. Grandpa waited. Finally, Justin, giving up, said, "Well, all right."

"Let's do it together," Grandpa said. "You on the other side."

Grandpa helped him smooth the bottom sheet and tuck it under the mattress at the head and foot of the bed. Then he put on the top sheet and blanket and smoothed them carefully.

"Now, let's tuck those under the mattress only at the foot of the bed," he said.

"That's really neat, Grandpa," Justin said, impressed.

"That's not it, yet. We want it to stay neat, don't we? Now watch." Grandpa carefully folded the covers in equal triangles and tucked them so that they made a neat corner at the end of the mattress. "Now do your side exactly the way I did mine."

Soon Justin was in bed. When Grandpa tucked him in, he asked, "How does it feel?"

Justin flexed his toes and ankles. "Nice. Snug."

"Like a bug in a rug?"

Justin laughed. Then Grandpa said, "That's how a man makes a bed."

Still laughing, Justin asked, "Who taught *you* how to make a bed? Your grandpa?"

"No. My grandma." Grandpa grinned and winked at Justin. "Good night."

Justin lay listening to the winds whispering in the trees. Out of his window in the darkness he saw lightning bugs flashing, heard crickets chirping. But before the first hoot of an owl, he was fast asleep.

THE SUN BEAMED down and sweat rolled off Justin as
he rode on with Grandpa, looking for broken wires in the
fence. They were well away from the house, on the far side
of the ranch. Flies buzzed around the horses and now
gnats swarmed in clouds just above their heads. The
prairie resounded with songs of the bluebirds, the
bobwhite quails, and the mockingbirds mimicking them all.
The cardinal's song, as lovely as any, included a whistle.

Justin thought of Anthony and how Anthony
whistled for Pepper, his dog.

It was well past noon and Justin was hungry. Soon
they came upon a small, well-built shed, securely locked.
Nearby was a small stream. Grandpa reined in his horse.
When he and Justin dismounted, they hitched the horses,
and unsaddled them.

"We'll have our lunch here," Grandpa said. Justin was surprised when Grandpa took black iron pots, other cooking utensils, and a table from the shed. Justin helped him remove some iron rods that Grandpa carefully placed over a shallow pit. These would hold the pots. Now Justin understood why Grandpa had brought uncooked food. They were going to cook outside.

First they collected twigs and cow dung. Grandpa called it cowchips. "These," Grandpa said, holding up a dried brown pad, "make the best fuel. Gather them up."

There were plenty of chips left from the cattle that had fed there in winter. Soon they had a hot fire.

Justin watched as Grandpa carefully washed his hands and then began to cook their lunch.

"When I was a boy about your age, I used to go with my father on short runs with cattle. "We'd bring them down from the high country onto the plains."

"Did you stay out all night?"

"Sometimes. And that was the time I liked most. The cook often made for supper what I am going to make for lunch."

Grandpa put raisins into a pot with a little water and placed them over the fire. Justin was surprised when Grandpa put flour in a separate pan. He used his fist to make a hole right in the middle of the flour. In that hole he placed some shortening. Then he added water. With his long delicate fingers he mixed the flour, water, and shortening until he had a nice round mound of dough.

Soon smooth circles of biscuits sat in an iron skillet with a lid on top. Grandpa put the skillet on the fire with some of the red-hot chips scattered over the lid.

Justin was amazed. How could only those ingredients make good bread? But he said nothing as Grandpa put the chunks of smoked pork in a skillet and started them cooking. Soon the smell was so delicious, Justin could hardly wait.

Finally Grandpa suggested that Justin take the horses to drink at the stream. "Keep your eyes open and don't step on any snakes."

Justin knew that diamondback rattlers sometimes lurked around. They were dangerous. He must be careful. He watered Black first.

While watering Pal, he heard rustling in the grass. His heart pounded. He heard the noise again. He wanted to run, but was too afraid. He looked around carefully. There were two black eyes staring at him. He tried to pull Pal away from the water, but Pal refused to stop drinking. Then Justin saw the animal. It had a long tail like a rat's. But it was as big as a cat. Then he saw something crawling on its back. They were little babies, hanging on as the animal ran.

A mama opossum and her babies, he thought, and was no longer afraid.

By the time the horses were watered, lunch was ready. *"M-mm-m,"* Justin said as he reached for a plate. The biscuits were golden brown, yet fluffy inside. And the sizzling pork was now crisp. Never had he eaten stewed raisins before.

"Grandpa, I didn't know you could cook like this," Justin said when he had tasted the food. "I didn't know men could cook so good."

"Why, Justin, some of the best cooks in the world are men."

Justin remembered the egg on the floor and his rice burning. The look he gave Grandpa revealed his doubts.

"It's true," Grandpa said. "All the cooks on the cattle trail were men. In hotels and restaurants they call them chefs."

"How did you make these biscuits?"

"That's a secret. One day I'll let you make some."

"Were you a cowboy, Grandpa?"

"I'm still a cowboy."

"No, you're not."

"Yes, I am. I work with cattle, so I'm a cowboy."

"You know what I mean. The kind who rides bulls, broncobusters. That kind of cowboy."

"No, I'm not that kind. But I know some."

"Are they famous?"

"No, but I did meet a real famous Black cowboy once. When I was eight years old, my grandpa took me to meet his friend Bill Pickett. Bill Pickett was an old man then. He had a ranch in Oklahoma."

"Were there lots of Black cowboys?"

"Yes. Lots of them. They were hard workers, too. They busted broncos, branded calves, and drove cattle. My grandpa tamed wild mustangs."

"Bet they were famous."

"Oh, no. Some were. Bill Pickett created the sport of bulldogging. You'll see that at the rodeo. One cowboy named Williams taught Rough Rider Teddy Roosevelt how to break horses; and another one named Clay taught Will Rogers, the comedian, the art of roping." Grandpa offered Justin the last biscuit.

Bill Pickett

Jessie Stahl

When they had finished their lunch they led the horses away from the shed to graze. As they watched the horses, Grandpa went on, "Now, there were some more very famous Black cowboys. Jessie Stahl. They say he was the best rider of wild horses in the West."

"How could he be? Nobody ever heard about him. I didn't."

"Oh, there're lots of famous Blacks you never hear or read about. You ever hear about Deadwood Dick?"

Justin laughed. "No."

"There's another one. His real name was Nate Love. He could outride, outshoot anyone. In Deadwood City in the Dakota Territory, he roped, tied, saddled, mounted, and rode a wild horse faster than anyone. Then in the shooting match, he hit the bull's-eye every time. The people named him Deadwood Dick right on the spot. Enough about cowboys, now. While the horses graze, let's clean up here and get back to our men's work."

Nate Love

Justin felt that Grandpa was still teasing him, the way he had in Justin's room when he had placed his hand on Justin's shoulder. There was still the sense of shame whenever the outburst about

women's work and the tears were remembered.

As they cleaned the utensils and dishes, Justin asked, "Grandpa, you think housework is women's work?"

"Do you?" Grandpa asked quickly.

"I asked you first, Grandpa."

"I guess asking you that before I answer is unfair. No, I don't. Do you?"

"Well, it seems easier for them," Justin said as he splashed water all over, glad he was outside.

"Easier than for me?"

"Well, not for you, I guess, but for me, yeah."

"Could it be because you don't know how?"

"You mean like making the bed and folding the clothes."

"Yes." Grandpa stopped and looked at Justin. "Making the bed is easy now, isn't it? All work is that way. It doesn't matter who does the work, man or woman, when it needs to be done. What matters is that we try to learn how to do it the best we can in the most enjoyable way."

"I don't think I'll ever like housework," Justin said, drying a big iron pot.

"It's like any other kind of work. The better you do it, the easier it becomes, and we seem not to mind doing things that are easy."

With the cooking rods and all the utensils put away, they locked the shed and went for their horses.

"Now, I'm going to let you do the cinches again. You'll like that."

There's that teasing again, Justin thought. "Yeah. That's a man's work," he said, and mounted Black.

"There are some good horsewomen. You'll see them at the rodeo." Grandpa mounted Pal. They went on their way, riding along silently, scanning the fence.

Finally Justin said, "I was just kidding, Grandpa." Then without planning to, he said, "I bet you don't like boys who cry like babies."

"Do I know any boys who cry like babies?"

"Aw, Grandpa, you saw me crying."

"Oh, I didn't think you were crying like a baby. In your room, you mean? We all cry sometime."

"You? Cry, Grandpa?"

"Sure."

They rode on, with Grandpa marking his map. Justin remained quiet, wondering what could make a man like Grandpa cry.

As if knowing Justin's thoughts, Grandpa said, "I remember crying when you were born."

"Why? Didn't you want me?"

"Oh, yes. You were the most beautiful baby. But, you see, your grandma, Beth, had just died. When I held you I was flooded with joy. Then I thought, *Grandma will never see this beautiful boy.* I cried."

The horses wading through the grass made the only sound in the silence. Then Grandpa said, "There's an old saying, son. 'The brave hide their fears, but share their tears.' Tears bathe the soul."

Justin looked at his grandpa. Their eyes caught. A warmth spread over Justin and he lowered his eyes. He wished he could tell his grandpa all he felt, how much he loved him.

Justin's grandfather told him that the better you do something, the easier it is to do it. Tell why you agree or disagree.

By the end of the story, how do you think Justin feels about household chores? Explain your answer.

Do you think Justin will be able to go home and make a batch of biscuits? Why or why not?

WRITE   Does any character in this story remind you of someone you know? Write a paragraph comparing the character and the person who is like the character.

WORDS about the Author:
Mildred Pitts Walter

Mildred Pitts Walter was born in Louisiana, the youngest of seven children. Her father was a log cutter, and the family lived in two small houses owned by the lumber company. They used one house for sleeping and the other for daytime activities such as cooking and washing. The yards of the two houses were used as a community meeting place. On Saturday nights, the neighbors gathered there for food, games, singing, storytelling, and dancing.

Young Mildred was eager for school to start each fall so she could read the school's library books. She spent the summers of her school years working to earn money for college. She was graduated from Southern University in Scotlandville, Louisiana.

After graduation, Mildred taught kindergarten and elementary grades. She also helped organize a program called Head Start. This program prepares

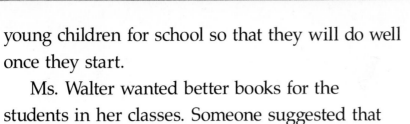

young children for school so that they will do well once they start.

Ms. Walter wanted better books for the students in her classes. Someone suggested that she write the books herself, so she did!

Mildred Walter writes about what she knows well—family life, problems at school, and the struggles of black people. Her years spent as a teacher help her write about the characters in her stories. She tries to understand her characters just as she tried to understand her students. She feels that an author needs to notice details that other people may miss.

As a child, Mildred was allowed to make choices, and learned to live with the results. Now she uses this idea in her stories. The characters in her books often face difficult choices, as Justin did in "Spending Time with Grandpa." When her characters use courage to make a choice, they are able to make changes in their lives.

Versos sencillos

by José Martí

illustrated by Edward Martinez

Tiene el leopardo un abrigo
en su monte seco y pardo:
Y yo tengo más que el leopardo
porque tengo un buen amigo.

Tiene el señor presidente
un jardín con una fuente,
y un tesoro en oro y trigo:
tengo más, tengo un amigo.

Simple Verses

(English version by María Elena Calderón)

The leopard has shelter
In the mountain dry and brown:
I have more than the leopard—
I have a good friend.

The president
Has a garden with a fountain,
And a treasure of wheat and gold:
I have more, I have a friend.

214

Learning About Yourself

The title of the theme you have just read is "Learning About Yourself." Think about Justin, and think about the poem. What did you learn about yourself from reading these selections?

WRITER'S WORKSHOP

In "Justin and the Best Biscuits in the World," you read about real-life cowboys. Choose one of the cowboys mentioned. Write a friendly letter to him, asking questions about what his life is like.

Writer's Choice: Write one or two paragraphs about something you have learned with the help of a friend. Or write about things you think older people can teach you. Organize your ideas, write, and then share your writing.

215

CONNECTIONS

Multicultural Connection

Friends Are People Who Care

When Antonia Novello was a child in Puerto Rico, she had a health problem. Every summer, she spent time in the hospital. She came to think of her kind doctors as friends.

Antonia decided to be a doctor herself. Her parents encouraged her through years of hard study. She became a doctor and began running health care programs that helped millions of people.

Dr. Novello then became the surgeon general of the United States. Like the doctors who were her childhood friends, she cared for others through her work.

Write a paragraph about a person who helps others. Publish your work in a class book titled "A Friend Is Someone Who Cares."

Dr. Antonia Novello

Puerto Rico

Social Studies Connection

Special People—Special Places

Antonia Novello came from Puerto Rico. With your classmates, find out some interesting facts about this island. Use the facts to make a collage of pictures and words that tell about this special place.

Health Connection

Staying Healthy

Think about how Antonia Novello helped people stay healthy. Then make a poster that shows some tips for staying healthy. Share your poster with your classmates.

UNIT THREE

Adventures

Adventure and mystery may be as far away as Peru or as near as a picture you paint. As you read the selections in this unit, look for the different ways the authors and illustrators share adventure. What does Allen Say tell about an Asian American family's camping adventure? How does Paul Sierra use paint to create mystery? This unit will give you a chance to find out.

THEMES

PICNIC WITH PIGGINS

by Jane Yolen

The picnic with Piggins has been delightful until . . . CRASH! SPLASH! Rexy, one of the Reynard kits, disappears, leaving baffling clues. Only Piggins can decode the curious note and unravel the mystery.

Award-Winning Author

Harcourt Brace Library Book

MUSH!

Across Alaska in the World's Longest Sled-Dog Race

by Patricia Seibert

This is the true story of the Iditarod Trail Sled-Dog Race. The book describes the history of the race and the challenges the racers and the dog teams face.

Notable Children's Trade Book in Social Studies

Harcourt Brace Library Book

HAIL TO MAIL

by Samuel Yakovlevich Marshak

This poem salutes travel, adventure, and mail. Join a letter as it follows John Peck from New York City to the ends of the earth.

Parents' Choice Honor

ON THE DAY YOU WERE BORN

by Debra Frasier

This book celebrates the relationship between the earth and its people. It's a song about the moon, the ocean, and all human life.

Parents' Choice Book

Notable Children's Trade Book in Social Studies

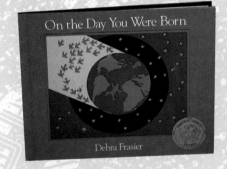

BLAST OFF TO EARTH!

by Loreen Leedy

This book takes you to a place where there are four oceans, seven continents, and countless mountains, deserts, and forests— our own planet.

Parents' Choice Honor

221

THEME

Picture This!

Each day, you face adventures, although you usually don't think about them. They can be adventures that you experience alone or with others. The unusual adventures in the legend and the play that follow should make you smile and laugh.

CONTENTS

223

The Legend of
the Indian Paintbrush

 retold and illustrated by
Tomie dePaola

♡ DE PAOLA

Many years ago
when the People traveled the Plains
and lived in a circle of teepees,
there was a boy who was smaller
than the rest of the children in the tribe.
No matter how hard he tried,
he couldn't keep up with the other boys
who were always riding, running, shooting their bows,
and wrestling to prove their strength.
Sometimes his mother and father worried for him.

But the boy, who was called Little Gopher,
was not without a gift of his own.
From an early age, he made toy warriors
from scraps of leather and pieces of wood
and he loved to decorate smooth stones
with the red juices from berries
he found in the hills.
The wise shaman of the tribe understood
that Little Gopher had a gift that was special.
"Do not struggle, Little Gopher.
Your path will not be the same as the others.
They will grow up to be warriors.
Your place among the People will be remembered
for a different reason."

And in a few years
when Little Gopher was older,
he went out to the hills alone
to think about becoming a man,
for this was the custom of the tribe.
And it was there that a Dream-Vision came to him.

The sky filled with clouds and out of them
came a young Indian maiden and an old grandfather.
She carried a rolled-up animal skin
and he carried a brush made of fine animal hairs
and pots of paints.

The grandfather spoke.
"My son, these are the tools
by which you shall become great among your People.
You will paint pictures of the deeds of the warriors
and the visions of the shaman,
and the People shall see them and remember them forever."

The maiden unrolled a pure white buckskin
and placed it on the ground.
"Find a buckskin as white as this," she told him.
"Keep it and one day you will paint a picture
that is as pure as the colors
in the evening sky."

And as she finished speaking, the clouds cleared
and a sunset of great beauty filled the sky.
Little Gopher looked at the white buckskin
and on it he saw colors as bright and beautiful
as those made by the setting sun.

Then the sun slowly sank behind the hills,
the sky grew dark,
and the Dream-Vision was over.
Little Gopher returned to the circle of the People.

The next day he began to make soft brushes
from the hairs of different animals
and stiff brushes from the hair of the horses' tails.
He gathered berries and flowers
and rocks of different colors
and crushed them to make his paints.

He collected the skins of animals,
which the warriors brought home from their hunts.
He stretched the skins on wooden frames
and pulled them until they were tight.

And he began to paint pictures . . .

Of great hunts . . . .

Of great deeds . . .

Of great Dream-Visions . . .
So that the People would always remember.

But even as he painted,
Little Gopher sometimes longed
to put aside his brushes
and ride out with the warriors.
But always he remembered his Dream-Vision
and he did not go with them.

Many months ago,
he had found his pure white buckskin,
but it remained empty
because he could not find the colors of the sunset.
He used the brightest flowers,
the reddest berries,
and the deepest purples from the rocks,
and still his paintings never satisfied him.
They looked dull and dark.

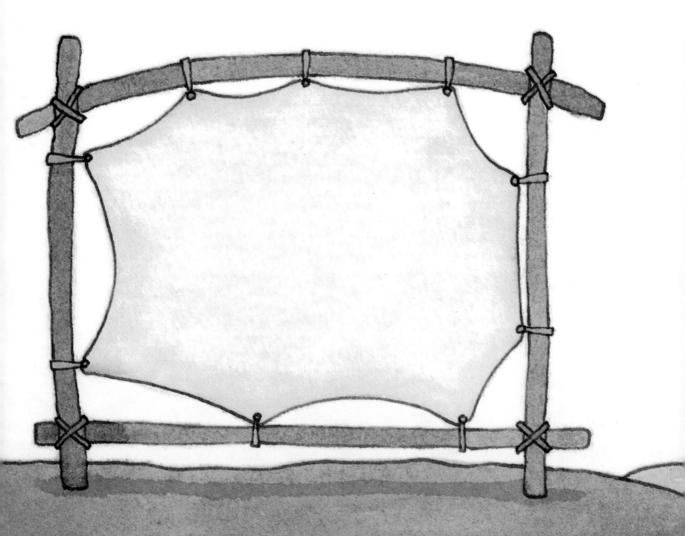

He began to go to the top of a hill each evening
and look at the colors that filled the sky
to try and understand how to make them.
He longed to share the beauty of his Dream-Vision
with the People.

But he never gave up trying,
and every morning when he awoke
he took out his brushes and his pots of paints
and created the stories of the People
with the tools he had.

One night as he lay awake,
he heard a voice calling to him.
"Because you have been faithful to the People
and true to your gift,
you shall find the colors you are seeking.
Tomorrow take the white buckskin
and go to the place
where you watch the sun in the evening.
There on the ground you will find what you need."

The next evening as the sun began to go down,
Little Gopher put aside his brushes
and went to the top of the hill
as the colors of the sunset spread across the sky.

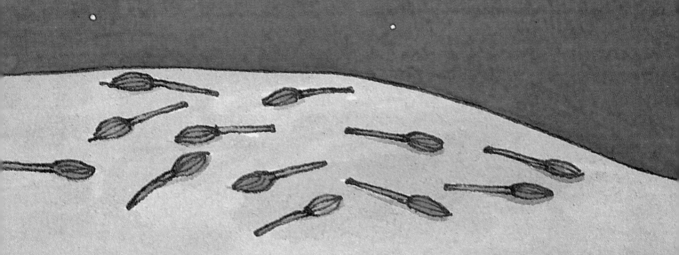

And there, on the ground all around him,
were brushes filled with paint,
each one a color of the sunset.
Little Gopher began to paint quickly and surely,
using one brush, then another.

And as the colors in the sky began to fade,
Little Gopher gazed at the white buckskin
and he was happy.

He had found the colors of the sunset.
He carried his painting down
to the circle of the People,
leaving the brushes on the hillside.

And the next day, when the People awoke,
the hill was ablaze with color,
for the brushes had taken root in the earth
and multiplied into plants
of brilliant reds, oranges and yellows.

And every spring from that time,
the hills and meadows burst into bloom.

And every spring,
the People danced and sang the praises
of Little Gopher who had painted for the People.

And the People no longer called him Little Gopher,
but He-Who-Brought-the-Sunset-to-the-Earth.

What does Tomie dePaola want you to learn
from Little Gopher?

How does the Dream-Vision change Little
Gopher's life?

WRITE   Little Gopher has a special talent.
Write a paragraph telling about someone's
special talents. Your paragraph can be
about you or about someone you know.

a Note from the Author:

Tomie dePaola

The lovely red, orange, yellow (and even pink) Indian Paintbrush blooms in Wyoming, Texas, and the high plains, and has many stories connected with its origin. The story of the Native American artist and his desire to paint the sunset was meaningful to me as an artist. (There are many times when I wish I could go out on a hill and find brushes filled with exactly the colors I need.)

The idea for doing a book on this wildflower came from my good friend Pat Henry after she had seen my book *The Legend of the Bluebonnet*, which is the story of the Texas state flower. Pat is from Wyoming where the Indian Paintbrush is the state flower.

Carolyn Sullivan from Austin, Texas, had recently sent me a copy of *Texas Wildflowers, Stories and Legends*. Carolyn is a teacher in the Austin area, and in 1965 this collection was made available to teachers there for use with a unit on Texas trees and wildflowers. She too had read the bluebonnet book and knew of my interest in folktale and legend. The Indian Paintbrush is a familiar flower to Texans and in the book I came across a brief and interesting account of how the wildflower got its name.

AWARD-WINNING
AUTHOR

PADDINGTON PAINTS A PICTURE

from PADDINGTON ON STAGE
adapted by Alfred Bradley and Michael Bond • illustrated by Peggy Fortnum

CAST OF CHARACTERS

MR. BROWN	MRS. BIRD	MRS. BROWN	JUDY
PADDINGTON	MISS BLACK	JONATHAN	MAN
MR. GRUBER			

PROPS

In the Browns'
sitting room:
    A few chairs
    Table
    Easel
For scene II:
    Suitcase
In Mr. Gruber's shop:
    Chair
    Sign saying "Antiques"
    Thermos flask, two mugs and a bun
    Pile of bric-a-brac, china, books, toys
    Half-restored "painting"

In the sitting room, for scenes III and IV:
    Very messy painting
    Paintbrush
    Paints—red and green
    Marmalade jar
    Spoon
    Palette (can be made from cardboard)
    Three empty bottles, painted to look as
    if they contain paint remover, ketchup
    and mustard
    Handkerchief
    Washing-up liquid
    Slip of paper for cheque

In this play the easel with Mr. Brown's painting should be placed near the centre of the stage so that Paddington has plenty of room to work on it. We don't need to see the painting, as it will be facing away from us until Miss Black brings it back at the end of the play. Of course, the tomato ketchup and mustard and paint remover should not be real (use empty bottles painted to look full), and the painting should be done beforehand so that it is dry for the performance. The painting should look as messy as you can make it.

When we get to Mr. Gruber's shop, all that we need to see is a pile of oddments with a notice saying "Antiques." Mr. Gruber should have a chair to sit on, a half-cleaned picture with a boat on one side and part of a lady's face on the other, a Thermos flask and two mugs.

Scene One

[*The Browns' sitting room.* MR. BROWN *is getting ready to go to work as* PADDINGTON *comes in. The easel is standing with its back to the audience.*]

MR. BROWN   Hello, Paddington. What are your plans for today?

PADDINGTON   I think I might do some shopping, Mr. Brown. I like shopping.

MR. BROWN   You won't get lost?

PADDINGTON   No, I won't be going very far. Is your painting finished, Mr. Brown?

MR. BROWN   Yes. [*He looks at it.*] You know, I really think it's the best I've ever done.

PADDINGTON   I hope you win a prize.

MR. BROWN   Oh, I don't expect I shall. But it's fun. That's the important thing, I suppose. I must be off now. I'm late for work already. [*He goes to the door.*] Goodbye, Paddington. I'll see you tonight.

PADDINGTON   Goodbye, Mr. Brown.

[MR. BROWN *goes, and* PADDINGTON *takes a closer look at the painting.*]

I think I would enjoy painting. It looks *very* interesting.

259

Scene Two

[*Mr. Gruber's bric-a-brac shop in the Portobello Road. He is cleaning an oil painting when* PADDINGTON *arrives.*]

MR. GRUBER   Good morning. Can I help you?

PADDINGTON   [*putting down his suitcase*] I don't know really. I was out for a walk and your shop looked so nice, I thought I would like to see inside.

MR. GRUBER   Please have a look round, Mr. . . . er . . .

PADDINGTON   Brown. Paddington Brown. I come from Darkest Peru.

MR. GRUBER   Darkest Peru? How strange. I know Peru quite well. I spent a lot of my early life in South America.

PADDINGTON   Fancy that, Mr. . . . er . . .

MR. GRUBER   Gruber. Look . . . I've just made some cocoa, Mr. Brown. Would you care for a cup?

PADDINGTON   Ooh, yes, please.

MR. GRUBER   It's quite hot. I keep it in a vacuum.

PADDINGTON   [*amazed*] You keep your cocoa in a vacuum cleaner?

MR. GRUBER   No, Mr. Brown, a vacuum flask. [*He pours some cocoa and hands it to* PADDINGTON.] There's nothing like a chat over a bun and a cup of cocoa.

PADDINGTON   A bun as well! [*They sit down to enjoy their elevenses.*[1]] What were you doing when I came into the shop, Mr. Gruber?

MR. GRUBER   I was cleaning a painting. [*He picks it up.*] Now, what do you think of that?

---

[1]elevenses: a snack taken in the middle of the morning

PADDINGTON [*looking at it*] It's a puzzle, Mr. Gruber. One half is a boat and the other half is a lady in a large hat.

MR. GRUBER There you are. I'd like your opinion on it, Mr. Brown.

PADDINGTON It doesn't seem to be one thing or the other.

MR. GRUBER Ah! It isn't at the moment. But just you wait until I've cleaned it! I gave five shillings[2] for that painting years and years ago, when it was just a picture of a sailing ship. And what do you think? When I started to clean it the other day, all the paint began to come off and I discovered that there was another painting underneath. [*confidentially*] It could be an old master.

---

[2]five shillings: British money, worth less than fifty cents

PADDINGTON   An old master? It looks like an old lady to me.

MR. GRUBER   [*laughs*] What I mean is, it could be very valuable. It could be by a famous painter.

PADDINGTON   That sounds interesting. Very interesting indeed. [*He gets up, his mind obviously elsewhere.*] I'll have to be going now, Mr. Gruber. Thank you for the elevenses.

MR. GRUBER   Is anything the matter, Mr. Brown?

PADDINGTON   No, Mr. Gruber. I've had an idea, that's all. [*mysteriously, as he makes to leave*] I may come into some money soon.

MR. GRUBER   Good day, Mr. Brown. I shall look forward to that. [*He watches* PADDINGTON *go.*] Come into some money! I wonder what he meant by that?

Scene Three

[*The Browns' sitting room.* PADDINGTON *comes in, looks round carefully. He takes a bottle of paint remover from his coat pocket. He soaks a handkerchief in paint remover and rubs it over the painting. He stands back to look and, horrified by what he sees, decides to have another try. He is giving the painting a vigorous scrub when* MRS. BIRD *enters.*]

MRS. BIRD   Now, Paddington, what are you up to? I thought you were out shopping.

PADDINGTON   I was. But I'm not any more. [*gloomily*] I wish I still was.

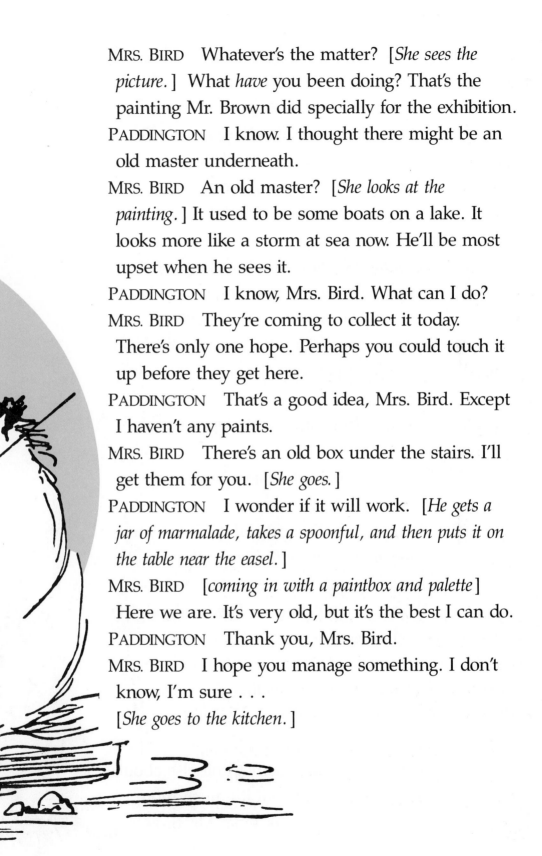

MRS. BIRD   Whatever's the matter? [*She sees the picture.*] What *have* you been doing? That's the painting Mr. Brown did specially for the exhibition.

PADDINGTON   I know. I thought there might be an old master underneath.

MRS. BIRD   An old master? [*She looks at the painting.*] It used to be some boats on a lake. It looks more like a storm at sea now. He'll be most upset when he sees it.

PADDINGTON   I know, Mrs. Bird. What can I do?

MRS. BIRD   They're coming to collect it today. There's only one hope. Perhaps you could touch it up before they get here.

PADDINGTON   That's a good idea, Mrs. Bird. Except I haven't any paints.

MRS. BIRD   There's an old box under the stairs. I'll get them for you. [*She goes.*]

PADDINGTON   I wonder if it will work. [*He gets a jar of marmalade, takes a spoonful, and then puts it on the table near the easel.*]

MRS. BIRD   [*coming in with a paintbox and palette*] Here we are. It's very old, but it's the best I can do.

PADDINGTON   Thank you, Mrs. Bird.

MRS. BIRD   I hope you manage something. I don't know, I'm sure . . .

[*She goes to the kitchen.*]

PADDINGTON   [*Holding the brush at arm's length, he considers the canvas.*] Uh, huh. [*He squeezes a tube of red paint on the palette, then he does the same with a green tube. He begins to paint boldly. Although we can't see the painting, it is obvious that he is making a mess.*] That looks better! [*Throughout this painting scene* PADDINGTON *occasionally touches the brush to his face, without realizing he is giving himself red and green spots. He dabs at the painting, absent-mindedly dipping his brush into the marmalade, and then decides to experiment. First he adds some mustard, and then the contents of a washing-up liquid squeezer and a bottle of tomato ketchup.*] There's one thing about painting, it's fun. [*He makes a huge mess of it.* MISS BLACK *arrives to collect the picture and knocks at the front door.* PADDINGTON *puts down his brush and goes to the door.*]

MISS BLACK   Good afternoon. I believe Mr. Brown has a painting for our exhibition.

PADDINGTON   Oh, yes. That's right. I'll get it for you. [*He goes back, gives the painting a finishing dab, wipes the brush on his hat, and takes the painting to the front door.*]

MISS BLACK   Thank you very much. The final judging takes place this afternoon.

PADDINGTON   The *final* judging?

MISS BLACK   Yes, we shall be awarding the prizes today. I expect you will hear the results later this evening. Goodbye. [*She goes.*]

PADDINGTON   Goodbye. There's something else about painting—it's fun while it lasts, but it's much more difficult than it looks. I can't think what Mr. Brown will say . . .

264

Scene Four

[*Later that day. The* BROWN *family is in the sitting room after dinner.*]

MRS. BROWN   Would you like a cup of cocoa, Paddington?
PADDINGTON   No, thank you.
MRS. BROWN   Are you all right?

PADDINGTON   Yes, I thank so, think you. I mean, I
  think so, thank you.

MRS. BROWN   Nothing on your mind?

PADDINGTON   No.

JONATHAN   How about a bull's-eye?[3]

PADDINGTON   No, thank you. I think I'll just go and
  have a rest for a bit. [*He goes out of the room.*]

MRS. BROWN   I do hope he's all right, Henry. He
  hardly touched his dinner, and that's not like him at
  all. And he seemed to have some funny red spots all
  over his face.

JONATHAN   Red spots! I wonder if it's measles. I hope
  he's given it to me, whatever it is. Then I will be able
  to stay away from school.

JUDY   Well, he's got green ones as well. I distinctly
  saw them.

MR. BROWN   Green ones! I wonder if he's sickening for
  something? If they're not gone in the morning, we'd
  better send for the doctor.

JONATHAN   They're judging the paintings today, aren't
  they, Dad?

MR. BROWN   Yes, they took mine away this afternoon.

JONATHAN   Do you think you'll win a prize?

MRS. BROWN   No one will be more surprised than
  your father if he does. He's never won a prize yet.

MR. BROWN   It took me a long while but I don't
  suppose I'll be any luckier than last time. The lady who
  collected it this afternoon told Paddington that the results
  would be made known today, so we'll soon know.

---

[3]bull's-eye: very hard round candy

JUDY   I wonder if he's feeling any better? [*She goes out.*]

JONATHAN   Perhaps they have *green* measles in Darkest Peru.

[*There is a knock at the front door. MRS. BIRD goes to answer it.*]

MRS. BIRD   Who can that be?

[MRS. BIRD *opens the door. MISS BLACK is waiting outside. She has a MAN with her. He is carrying Mr. Brown's painting, still with its back to the audience.*]

MISS BLACK   Good evening. Is Mr. Brown in?

MAN   We've come about the painting he entered for our competition.

MRS. BIRD   Oh, dear. Will you come this way, please? [*She ushers them into the room.*]

MAN   Mr. Brown?

MR. BROWN   That's right.

MAN   I'm the President of the Art Society, and this is Miss Black, who was one of the judges of the competition.

MR. BROWN   How do you do.

MAN   I've some news for you, Mr. Brown.

PADDINGTON   [*offstage*] Oooooh!

MISS BLACK   Good gracious! What was that?

MAN   It sounded like a cow mooing somewhere.

MRS. BROWN   I think it's only a bear oooohing.

MAN   Oh! Er . . . Mr. Brown, as I was saying,
the judges decided that your painting was most
unusual . . .

MRS. BIRD   It certainly was.

MAN   And they have all agreed to award you the first
prize.

MR. BROWN   The *first* prize?

MISS BLACK   Yes, they thought your painting showed
great imagination.

MR. BROWN   [*pleased*] Did they now?

MAN   It made great use of marmalade chunks.

THE BROWNS   [*chorus*] Marmalade chunks!

MAN   Yes, indeed. I don't think I've ever come across
anything quite like it before. [*He places the painting on
the easel facing the audience. It is, to say the least, unusual,
and there are several real marmalade chunks sticking to it.*]

MRS. BROWN   I didn't know you were interested in
abstract art, Henry.

MR. BROWN   Nor did I!

[PADDINGTON *and* JUDY *put their heads round the door.*]

MAN   [*He removes a marmalade chunk with a flourish and
swallows it.*] It not only looks good—it tastes good!

MISS BLACK   What are you calling it?

MR. BROWN   Where's Paddington?

MISS BLACK   Where's Paddington? What a funny title!

MAN   Well, sir, my congratulations! We'll be wanting
the painting back in a day or so to put into the
exhibition, but I'll leave it with you for the moment.
Just one more thing . . . your prize. [*He hands over a
cheque.*] £10.[4]

---

[4]£10: 10 pounds; about fifteen American dollars

MISS BLACK   May I ask what you will do with it, Mr. Brown?

MR. BROWN   [*wearily*] I think perhaps I'd better give it to a certain Home for Retired Bears in South America.

MAN   Oh, really? Well, we must be getting along.

[*As they leave,* PADDINGTON *falls into the room.* JUDY *follows him in.*]

MRS. BIRD   Well, Paddington. The secret's out. Now, what have you got to say for yourself?

PADDINGTON   [*Crosses to the painting. He removes a marmalade chunk and goes to eat it.*] I think it looks good enough to eat, Mr. Brown! [*He turns it up the other way.*] But I think they might have put it the right way up. After all, it's not every day a bear wins first prize in a painting competition.

CURTAIN

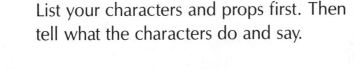

If you were one of the judges, how would you rate Paddington's painting? Explain why.

Why does Paddington change Mr. Brown's painting? How does he try to correct his mistake?

How does the Brown family feel about Paddington? How do you know?

WRITE   Make up a new ending for this play. List your characters and props first. Then tell what the characters do and say.

Picture This!

In the selections in this theme, the painters use unusual materials as their paints. In each case, these "paints" help make the paintings special. Which do you think is more important—the painter or the paints? Why?

WRITER'S WORKSHOP

Picture in your mind your favorite story character. Imagine that he or she has come into your world. Write a story about an experience or adventure the character might have.

Writer's Choice:

Imagine that you want to paint a picture but have no paints. Describe what you might use to paint a landscape. Or write about something else that interests you. Plan how to share your writing.

T H E M E

Mysteries to Solve

Some adventures involve a mystery. Sometimes a problem has to be solved or something lost must be found. Read the following story, riddle, and poems. Can you solve the mysteries in them?

C O N T E N T S

273

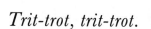

Trit-trot, trit-trot.

That is the sound of Piggins, the butler at 47 The Meadows, going up the stairs. He has shined the silver teapot so well he can see his snout in it.

UPSTAIRS Mrs. Reynard is in a terrible dither.

"I cannot find my diamond lavaliere," she says to her husband.

"Is it missing again?" Mr. Reynard asks. "Perhaps one of the servants took it." His whiskers twitch.

"*Our* Cook? *Our* Sara? *Our* Jane? Not possible," says Mrs. Reynard.

Mr. Reynard smiles widely enough so that his teeth show. "Perhaps the butler did it."

"*Our* Piggins?" Mrs. Reynard is clearly shocked. "He *finds* things. He does not *take* things."

"I know, my dear," says Mr. Reynard. "I was making a little joke. Look again and I will help you." He gets up from his chair.

They look and look. At last they find the necklace right where it belongs—in Mrs. Reynard's jewelry box.

ILLUSTRATED BY JANE DYER

BELOW STAIRS Cook has just removed the cake from the oven. The kitchen is sweet with its smell. Sara, the scullery maid, has scrubbed the pots and pans. She looks as if she needs a scrubbing herself. Upstairs Jane has finished setting the table. Everything is in its proper place.

IN THE DINING ROOM Piggins is pleased. The glasses sparkle. The silver gleams. Even the chandelier glitters like a thousand diamonds.

Ding-dong. That is the front door bell. Piggins goes to answer it. The dinner guests have started to arrive.

Inspector Bayswater and his friend Professor T. Ortoise are on the steps. The professor is telling a joke. Lord and Lady Ratsby alight from a carriage. They are arguing with the driver over the fare. Down the street comes the motorcar of the world-famous explorer Pierre Lapin and his three unmarried sisters. He honks the horn. *Aaaa-OOOO-ga. Aaaa-OOOO-ga.* His sisters scream with delight.

"Lovely weather," says the professor in the living room. He is famous for his conversation. His students all say proudly, "Professor T. Ortoise taught us."

Lord and Lady Ratsby eye the cheeses hungrily. They sample every cheese and even slip a few pieces into their pockets.

Inspector Bayswater takes out his pipe. He does not light it. The doctors have advised him not to smoke.

Pierre Lapin settles his sisters. "Do you want something to drink?" he asks them.

"Anything but tea," the eldest says. The other two giggle.

Mr. and Mrs. Reynard come into the room and smile warmly at their friends. They greet each of them by name. Everyone admires Mrs. Reynard's diamond lavaliere.

"You may wonder why I have asked you here this evening," says Mr. Reynard.

But no one *really* wonders. Mr. Reynard is a tinkerer. He loves to invite friends over to show off his latest invention.

Mr. Reynard surprises them. "Tonight I will say nothing about my inventions, though I do have one or two small new things." He waves his paw toward several strange contraptions in the corner of the room. "Tonight I want to tell you about—"

"Dinner is served," announces Piggins.

So two by two they go in to dinner. Lord and Lady Ratsby are so hungry they scamper on ahead. Slow but steady, the professor brings up the rear, the eldest Miss Lapin on his arm. It would simply not do to let Cook's wonderful food get cold.

When the shrimp soup has been served, Mr. Reynard smiles. "I have invited you to dinner tonight so that you can admire my wife's brand-new diamond necklace. And so you can hear the story of why we must sell it."

"Sell it?" The eldest Miss Lapin leans forward. "But it is so beautiful. How can you bear to part with it?"

"It must be worth a great deal of money," says Lady Ratsby. She fingers her own necklace, a simple gold chain.

"Yes, it *is* beautiful," says Mrs. Reynard. "And quite expensive. But . . ."

"But what?" asks the inspector. His professional interest has been aroused.

"There is a curse on the diamond!" says Mr. Reynard.

"*A curse!*" Everyone talks at once.

Mr. Reynard silences them by holding up his right paw. "Yes—a curse! The miner who found the diamond broke his arm. The cutter who shaped it broke all his tools. The store that sold the necklace burned down right after the sale."

"And you?" asks the professor, keeping the conversation going.

"Yes," says Pierre Lapin. "What has happened to you?"

Mrs. Reynard looks sad. "I have lost the lavaliere three times already. Sara broke a bowl and a glass. Cook's first cake flopped. The children have the fox pox. And—"

"Nothing serious has happened . . . yet," says Mr. Reynard. "But just in case, we have decided to sell the lavaliere as soon as possible. I know all of you are interested in gems, so I called you together tonight."

"We are interested indeed," says Lord Ratsby. *"What good timing!"*

Suddenly the lights go out.

A strange tinkling sound is heard.

There is a scramble of feet.

Several objects thud to the floor.

There is a high, squeaky scream.

In comes Piggins with a candle.

Lord Ratsby finds the light switch and turns on the glittering chandelier.

Professor T. Ortoise stands up.

Pierre Lapin sets the table aright.

Just then Mrs. Reynard clutches her throat. She screams.

"My diamond lavaliere. It is gone." She falls back in a faint.

Lady Ratsby points her finger at Piggins. "Perhaps the butler did it."

"Balderdash and poppycock," says Mr. Reynard. He turns to the inspector. "I cannot believe *our* Piggins did it. Can you find any clues to the real thief?"

The inspector examines the room. He searches everywhere. He finds a red thread near the door, crumbs on the table, and a little bit of dirt on the floor. He cannot find the diamond lavaliere.

"I am stumped," he says at last.

"Hummmmph!" snorts Lady Ratsby.

Professor T. Ortoise is at a loss for words for the first time in his life.

Pierre Lapin comforts his three sisters, who sniffle into their lace handkerchiefs.

Mrs. Reynard comes out of her faint.

Piggins smiles. "I, on the other hand, am not stumped. I know who has done it."

"Good show, Piggins," says Mr. Reynard. "Tell us everything. And I will record it with my latest invention."

"First there are the clues," says Piggins. "A piece of red thread near the door. A trail of cheese crumbs on the table. The tinkling sound we all heard. The scream."

"And the dirt on the floor?" asks the inspector.

"For that I shall have to speak sharply to Upstairs Jane," says Piggins, frowning. "There should be *no* dirt in this house."

"I do not understand the clues," says the professor. "Thread, crumbs, a tinkling sound, a scream."

"There is not one thief—but two," explains Piggins. "One to turn off the lights and make a commotion, and one to steal the diamond lavaliere."

"Oh," says Pierre Lapin. "I know all about making commotions. In my youth, I stole into a farmer's garden and made much too much noise."

"The clues," remind the Misses Lapin together.

Piggins continues. "Before everyone came into dinner, someone tied the red thread to the light switch. At a signal, the thread was pulled and the lights turned off. But the thread was pulled so hard, it broke. In the dark someone grabbed the necklace and stepped up onto the table, leaving a trail of cheese crumbs where no cheese had been served. The tinkling sound was the chandelier being disturbed. The scream was the signal that all was clear."

"Then that means . . . " says Inspector Bayswater.

"That the thieves are . . . " says the professor.

"None other than . . . " says Mr. Reynard.

"Lord and Lady Ratsby," finishes Piggins. "They knew about the diamond all along and planned to steal it at their very first chance."

"But where *is* the diamond?" asks the professor. "Inspector Bayswater looked everywhere."

"Yes," sneers Lord Ratsby. "Where is your precious diamond?"

Piggins smiles. "In plain sight." He steps on one of the chairs and reaches up into the glittering chandelier. He finds the necklace.

"I suspected the Ratsbys were broke," says the eldest Miss Lapin. "Lady Ratsby is wearing a simple gold chain. Usually she drips jewels."

"Catch them!" Mrs. Reynard cries, for the Ratsbys are trying to escape.

The eldest Miss Lapin sticks out her foot. She trips Lord Ratsby. The younger Misses Lapin jump on top of Lady Ratsby.

"Well done, Piggins," says Mr. Reynard.

"Well done, girls!" cries Mrs. Reynard.

"Curses!" says Lord Ratsby.

Professor T. Ortoise laughs. "Curses indeed! Perhaps, Reynard, the curse on your lavaliere is at its end."

The police are summoned and they take the Ratsbys away.

UPSTAIRS Mr. and Mrs. Reynard get ready for bed. Mrs. Reynard carefully wraps the diamond lavaliere in a velvet cloth. She puts it away in her jewelry box. "I hope the curse *is* ended," she says. "I would hate to part with my beautiful necklace."

Mr. Reynard nods and takes off his tie. "I knew the butler did not do it," he says.

"Not *our* Piggins," says Mrs. Reynard.

BELOW STAIRS Sara has cleaned the last of the dishes. She could do with a cleaning herself. Cook snoozes in her chair. And Jane, having swept up the dirt on the dining room floor, has set the kettle on the stove for one last cup of tea.

IN THE DINING ROOM Everything is quiet and clean. Piggins locks the front door at 47 The Meadows. He hears the kettle whistling.

It has been a long and interesting evening. Piggins is tired. Teapot in hand, he goes back down the stairs. *Trit-trot, trit-trot, trit-trot.*

Would you like to read more mystery stories about Piggins? Why or why not?

Is Piggins a real detective? What makes you think he is or isn't?

How does Piggins solve the mystery?

Would you want to be a member of the Reynards' staff? Give reasons for your answer.

WRITE What do you like or dislike about mystery stories? Write a paragraph telling how you feel.

WORDS FROM THE
AUTHOR *And The* ILLUSTRATOR:

Jane Yolen and Jane Dyer

Every story has a starting place, but it is often difficult to guess it. You may think that *Piggins* began with *Trit-trot, trit-trot* but actually it began with a series of mystery books, a television show, and an illustration of three bears.

The series of mystery books I mean were from England and star a detective named Lord Peter Wimsey. His butler, Bunter, assists him in every mystery he solves.

Written in the 1930s and 1940s by British author Dorothy Sayers, these books are particular favorites of mine, and I have read each of them many times.

The television show is a long-running series called *Upstairs, Downstairs*. It's about a British family in the late 1800s and early 1900s. The family has a butler, a cook, a messy young kitchen maid, an upstairs maid, and a house with a great many rooms. They are always holding formal dinner parties.

The illustration was shown to me during a writing class I was teaching. The young artist, Jane Dyer, had done work for textbooks and sticker books, but she had never illustrated a picture book before. I fell in love with one illustration showing three bears sitting down to a breakfast of porridge. They were elegantly dressed in their cozy little forest cottage.

Without really meaning to, I came up with an idea for a book: What about a . . . a pig butler named Piggins, dressed in a tuxedo, who works for a family in a fancy house and solves mysteries? When I asked Jane Dyer if she would like to try the illustrations she looked at me as if I were crazy.

"Would I?" she whispered in a soft voice. Then she almost shouted, "Oh, boy, WOULD I!"

And she did.

P.S. Here is a funny ending to the story. Four years after the first of the three PIGGINS books came out, I got a letter from a lady named Mrs. Ethel Piggins. She wondered if I had heard of her and if her name had given me the idea for my books. She said that I had met her daughter once years before. I didn't remember meeting her daughter and told her so. Several months later a young woman named Ms. Reynard asked me the same question. I hadn't ever met her before either. But sometimes the things you make up come true— in an odd sort of way.

Closed, I am a mystery
by Myra Cohn Livingston

AWARD-WINNING
AUTHOR

Closed, I am a mystery.
Open, I will always be
a friend with whom you think and see.

Closed, there's nothing I can say.
Open, we can dream and stray
to other worlds, far and away.

(A BOOK)

Hello Book!

by N. M. Bodecker
illustrated by Merle Nacht

Hello book!
What are you up to?
Keeping yourself to yourself,
shut in between your covers,
a prisoner high on a shelf.
Come in book!
What is your story?
Haven't you ever been read?
Did you think
         I would just pass by you,
And pick me a comic instead?
No way book!
I'm your reader.
I open you up. Set you free.
Listen, I know a secret!
Will you share
         your secrets with me?

AWARD-WINNING
AUTHOR

Would you like

by Lillian Morrison
illustrated by Michael Stiernagle

stories that surprise you
and/or hypnotize you,
a mystery, a history,
a volume to advise you
how to fix a motor,
build your own computer,
use a tape recorder,
get along with mother?
How about a voyage
into outer space,
romance with an Alien
of a future race?
Then dip in, dig in
grapple in with hooks,
dive in, delve in
GET INTO BOOKS.

Mysteries to Solve

The story, riddle, and poems you have just read all contain mysteries. A mystery can be solved by paying careful attention to the clues. Piggins points out things that he sees or hears. What are some other ways to find clues? Describe one.

Writer's Workshop

Everyone seemed to be sure that Piggins had not stolen the necklace, because he could be trusted. Write a paragraph explaining why it is important to be trusted.

Writer's Choice:
Write a paragraph about a favorite mystery. Or write a riddle or a mystery of your own. Choose an idea, write, and then share what you wrote.

The Great Outdoors

How does it feel to be outdoors with just
nature around you? How does it feel to
explore the outdoors with other people?
Think about your own feelings as you
read the story and the poems.

CONTENTS

AWARD-WINNING
AUTHOR AND
ILLUSTRATOR

THE LOST LAKE

ALLEN SAY

I went to live with Dad last summer.

Every day he worked in his room from morning to night, sometimes on weekends, too. Dad wasn't much of a talker, but when he was busy he didn't talk at all.

I didn't know anybody in the city, so I stayed home most of the time. It was too hot to play outside anyway. In one month I finished all the books I'd brought and grew tired of watching TV.

One morning I started cutting pictures out of old magazines, just to be doing something. They were pictures of mountains and rivers and lakes, and some showed people fishing and canoeing. Looking at them made me feel cool, so I pinned them up in my room.

Dad didn't notice them for two days. When he did, he looked at them one by one.

"Nice pictures," he said.

"Are you angry with me, Dad?" I asked, because he saved old magazines for his work.

"It's all right, Luke," he said. "I'm having this place painted soon anyway."

He thought I was talking about the marks I'd made on the wall.

That Saturday Dad woke me up early in the morning and told me we were going camping! I was wide awake in a second. He gave me a pair of brand-new hiking boots to try out. They were perfect.

In the hallway I saw a big backpack and a knapsack all packed and ready to go.

"What's in them, Dad?" I asked.

"Later," he said. "We have a long drive ahead of us."

In the car I didn't ask any more questions because Dad was so grumpy in the morning.

"Want a sip?" he said, handing me his mug. He'd never let me drink coffee before. It had lots of sugar in it.

"Where are we going?" I finally asked.

"We're off to the Lost Lake, my lad."

"How can you lose a lake?"

"No one's found it, that's how." Dad was smiling!
"Grandpa and I used to go there a long time ago. It
was our special place, so don't tell any of your
friends."

"I'll never tell," I promised. "How long are we
going to stay there?"

"Five days, maybe a week."

"We're going to sleep outside for a whole week?"

"That's the idea."

"Oh, boy!"

We got to the mountains in the afternoon.

"It's a bit of a hike to the lake, son," Dad said.

"I don't mind," I told him. "Are there any fish in the lake?"

"Hope so. We'll have to catch our dinner, you know."

"You didn't bring any food?"

"Of course not. We're going to live like true outdoorsmen."

"Oh . . ."

Dad saw my face and started to laugh. He must have been joking. I didn't think we were going very far anyway, because Dad's pack was so heavy I couldn't even lift it.

Well, Dad was like a mountain goat. He went straight up the trail, whistling all the while. But I was gasping in no time. My knapsack got very heavy and I started to fall behind.

Dad stopped for me often, but he wouldn't let me take off my pack. If I did I'd be too tired to go on, he said.

It was almost suppertime when we got to the lake.

The place reminded me of the park near Dad's apartment. He wasn't whistling or humming anymore.

"Welcome to the *Found* Lake," he muttered from the side of his mouth.

"What's wrong, Dad?"

"Do you want to camp with all these people around us?"

"I don't mind."

"Well, I do!"

"Are we going home?"

"Of course not!"

He didn't even take off his pack. He just turned and started to walk away.

Soon the lake was far out of sight.

Then it started to rain. Dad gave me a poncho and it kept me dry, but I wondered where we were going to sleep that night. I wondered what we were going to do for dinner. I wasn't sure about camping anymore.

I was glad when Dad finally stopped and set up the tent. The rain and wind beat against it, but we were warm and cozy inside. And Dad had brought food. For dinner we had salami and dried apricots.

"I'm sorry about the lake, Dad," I said.

He shook his head. "You know something, Luke? There aren't any secret places left in the world anymore."

"What if we go very far up in the mountains? Maybe we can find our own lake."

"There are lots of lakes up here, but that one was special."

"But we've got a whole week, Dad."

"Well, why not? Maybe we'll find a lake that's not on the map."

"Sure, we will!"

We started early in the morning. When the fog cleared we saw other hikers ahead of us. Sure enough, Dad became very glum.

"We're going cross-country, partner," he said.

"Won't we get lost?"

"A wise man never leaves home without his compass."

So we went off the trail. The hills went on and on. The mountains went on and on. It was kind of lonesome. It seemed as if Dad and I were the only people left in the world.

And then we hiked into a big forest.

At noontime we stopped by a creek and ate lunch and drank ice-cold water straight from the stream. I threw rocks in the water, and fish, like shadows, darted in the pools.

"Isn't this a good place to camp, Dad?"

"I thought we were looking for our lake."

"Yes, right . . ." I mumbled.

The forest went on and on.

"I don't mean to scare you, son," Dad said. "But we're in bear country. We don't want to surprise them, so we have to make a lot of noise. If they hear us, they'll just go away."

What a time to tell me! I started to shout as loudly

as I could. Even Dad wouldn't be able to beat off
bears. I thought about those people having fun back
at the lake. I thought about the creek, too, with all
those fish in it. That would have been a fine place to
camp. The Lost Lake hadn't been so bad either.

It was dark when we got out of the forest. We
built a fire and that made me feel better. Wild animals
wouldn't come near a fire. Dad cooked beef stroganoff
and it was delicious.

Later it was bedtime. The sleeping bag felt wonderful. Dad and I started to count the shooting stars, then I worried that maybe we weren't going to find our lake.

"What are you thinking about, Luke?" Dad asked.

"I didn't know you could cook like that," I said.

Dad laughed. "That was only freeze-dried stuff. When we get home, I'll cook you something really special."

"You know something, Dad? You seem like a different person up here."

"Better or worse?"

"A lot better."

"How so?"

"You talk more."

"I'll have to talk more often, then."

That made me smile. Then I slept.

Dad shook me awake. The sun was just coming up, turning everything all gold and orange and yellow. And there was the lake, right in front of us.

For a long time we watched the light change on the water, getting brighter and brighter. Dad didn't say a word the whole time. But then, I didn't have anything to say either.

After breakfast we climbed a mountain and saw our lake below us. There wasn't a sign of people anywhere. It really seemed as if Dad and I were all alone in the world.

I liked it just fine.

Would you have liked to go on the camping trip with Luke and his father? Explain why or why not.

When Luke and his father arrive at the lake, it is crowded with people. How would the story be different if they decided to stay there?

Luke is happy that his father talks more when they go hiking. Why does Luke not mind that they are silent when they look out on the lake at the end of the story?

WRITE Imagine that you are on vacation at a "lost" lake. Write a postcard to a friend, telling about the lake.

Words from the AUTHOR and ILLUSTRATOR:

Allen Say

I began *Lost Lake* by painting the pictures. I didn't really know what the story was going to be about until I was halfway through the art. This is how I work. I find my characters through the pictures. When the characters I'm drawing become real to me, then the story starts to take shape.

311

I had actually gone to a place called Lost Lake in my twenties when I came out of the army. A friend, who was a very outdoorsy person, took me there. I had done a lot of camping when I was in the army, so I wasn't very keen to go to this place in the Sierra Mountains, but I went with my friend. We had to trek six miles before we got to Lost Lake, and just as in the story, the area was full of people with radios and dirt bikes. It was noisy! I remembered that incident, and it became the kernel of the text.

I also wanted to write about the kind of father I wished I had had, but when I finished the story, I suddenly realized that the father in it is me. Maybe this was my way of apologizing to my daughter, because I didn't feel I was spending enough time with her. So, like my other stories, this one became very personal.

It can take a long time to do a picture book. One book, *El Chino,* took me eleven months to write, and during that period I had only one weekend off.

Although I haven't done it in a while, when I need time off in a quiet place, I go fly-fishing. I've fished in Iceland, Alaska, and Argentina. Now, because I'm so busy, I don't really have an outdoors life. I have to be content with taking walks.

PEOLE

by Charlotte Zolotow
illustrated by Andrea Eberbach

Some people talk and talk
and never say a thing.
Some people look at you
and birds begin to sing.

Some people laugh and laugh
and yet you want to cry.
Some people touch your hand
and music fills the sky.

Some PEOPLE

by Rachel Field
illustrated by
Andrea Eberbach

Isn't it strange some people make
  You feel so tired inside,
Your thoughts begin to shrivel up
  Like leaves all brown and dried!

But when you're with some other ones,
  It's stranger still to find
Your thoughts as thick as fireflies
  All shiny in your mind!

The Great Outdoors

In "The Lost Lake" and the poems you read, the writers seem to say that spending time with people you care about can be an adventure. Do you agree? Why or why not?

WRITER'S WORKSHOP

Would you recommend "The Lost Lake" to a friend? Write a review, telling whether you think other people would like it. Give your reasons.

Writer's Choice:
If you have ever gone camping, you might want to write about your camping trip. Or you might want to write about a place you would like to visit. Choose an idea, and write about it. Then share your writing.

315

CONNECTIONS

Multicultural Connection

Sierra's Mystery Picture

Look at the man in the painting. Who could he be? What is happening all around him? What might he do next?

Paul Sierra, the Chicago artist who painted this picture, has presented us with a mystery. We do not know where this scene is set. Could it show something that happened in Cuba, where the artist grew up?

We can't be sure. Only Sierra knows the answer, and he does not tell us. Like most artists, he wants his work to touch our feelings and make us think.

Paint a picture that creates a mood of mystery and adventure. Ask your classmates what your picture makes them think and feel.

Paul Sierra

Social Studies Connection

The Mysteries of Memory

Paul Sierra grew up in Cuba. Look at photographs of Cuba or another Caribbean island, and read about that place. Imagine that you are an artist from that island. Describe some memories that you would paint.

Cuban Coastline

Science Connection

A Place Like No Other

What place is shown in the scene that Paul Sierra painted? Draw or map an imaginary place where a mystery or an adventure might happen. Show what kinds of plants grow there, where people live, and what the weather is like. Then write about what might happen there.

Viñales Valley Cuba

GLOSSARY

The **pronunciation** of each word in this glossary is shown by a phonetic respelling in brackets; for example, [ə•fek′shən•it•lē]. An accent mark (′) follows the syllable with the most stress: [an•tēk′]. A secondary, or lighter, accent mark (′) follows a syllable with less stress: [fig′yər•hed′]. The key to other pronunciation symbols is below. You will find a shortened version of this key on alternate pages of the glossary.

Pronunciation Key*

a	add, map	m	move, seem	u	up, done
ā	ace, rate	n	nice, tin	û(r)	burn, term
â(r)	care, air	ng	ring, song	yo͞o	fuse, few
ä	palm, father	o	odd, hot	v	vain, eve
b	bat, rub	ō	open, so	w	win, away
ch	check, catch	ô	order, jaw	y	yet, yearn
d	dog, rod	oi	oil, boy	z	zest, muse
e	end, pet	ou	pout, now	zh	vision, pleasure
ē	equal, tree	o͝o	took, full	ə	the schwa,
f	fit, half	o͞o	pool, food		an unstressed
g	go, log	p	pit, stop		vowel representing
h	hope, hate	r	run, poor		the sound spelled
i	it, give	s	see, pass		a in *above*
ī	ice, write	sh	sure, rush		e in *sicken*
j	joy, ledge	t	talk, sit		i in *possible*
k	cool, take	th	thin, both		o in *melon*
l	look, rule	t̶h̶	this, bathe		u in *circus*

*Adapted entries, the Pronunciation Key, and the Short Key that appear on the following pages are reprinted from *HBJ School Dictionary*. Copyright © 1990 by Harcourt Brace & Company. Reprinted by permission of Harcourt Brace & Company.

A

accordion

apricot

antique   *Antique* comes from the Latin version of a word meaning "before." The Latin word later became the English word *ancient*. During the last century *antique* has come to mean "made long ago and of value." So some people collect old furniture, jewelry, and dishes in the hope they will one day be worth lots of money.

ab·sent·mind·ed [ab'sənt·mīn'did] *adj.* Forgetful; not paying attention: **My *absentminded* uncle forgot my birthday.**

ac·cor·di·on [ə·kôr'dē·ən] *n.* A musical instrument that is played by fingering a keyboard on one side and by squeezing large folds or bellows in and out on the opposite side: **The *accordion* is so large that the player uses straps to hold it.**

ac·cu·ra·cy [ak'yər·ə·sē] *n.* Correctness; having no mistakes: **Bruno does math with *accuracy.***

ad·ven·ture [ad·ven'chər] *n.* A thrilling experience; an exciting event: **Bill's dream was filled with *adventures* at sea.**

af·fec·tion·ate·ly [ə·fek'shən·it·lē] *adv.* With love and emotion: **Mother hugged us *affectionately* when we came home.**

an·ni·ver·sa·ry [an'ə·vûr'sə·rē] *n.* Usually a celebration of a day of the year to remember something important from the past: **Claudia attended a party for her aunt and uncle's wedding *anniversary.***

an·tique [an·tēk'] *n.* Something made long ago and valued for its age: **The *antiques* in our house are all over a hundred years old.**

a·part·ment [ə·pärt'mənt] *n.* A place someone lives in: **Lara lives in an *apartment* that has six rooms.**

a·pri·cot [ā'pri·kot *or* ap'ri·kot] *n.* A small, orange-colored fruit: **Sally ate two *apricots* for a snack.**

ar·gue [är'gyo͞o] *v.* **ar·gued, ar·gu·ing**   To fight by using words: **George and Alice are *arguing* loudly about who will sit in the fror seat.** *syn.* disagree

as•sem•bly [ə•sem′blē] *n.* In school, a gathering of students and teachers for educational or entertainment programs.

as•sign [ə•sīn′] *v.* **as•signed, as•sign•ing** To give someone a job or task to do: **The teacher** *assigned* **homework today.**

as•sur•ance [ə•shŏŏr′əns] *n.* Words or actions that make someone feel better or less afraid: **The child needed** *assurance* **that he was safe during the storm.**

au•di•ence [ô′dē•əns] *n.* A group of people who listen to and watch a performance: **The** *audience* **must be quiet so that everybody can enjoy the play.**

B

band [band] *n.* A group of musicians who get together to play their instruments, usually brass, percussion, and woodwinds.

base•ment [bās′mənt] *n.* The lowest floor of a house or building, partly below ground level: **We ran down into the** *basement* **when we heard the tornado warning.**

beck•on [bek′ən] *v.* **beck•oned, beck•on•ing** To signal or call to come over: **The teacher waved and** *beckoned* **the students into the classroom.**

bois•ter•ous [bois′tər•əs] *adj.* Noisy and wild: **The** *boisterous* **children made it hard to hear the TV.** *syns.* loud, excited

bound [bound] *v.* **bound•ed, bound•ing** To leap: **We saw the playful kitten** *bounding* **toward the fallen leaf.**

Braille [brāl] *n.* A system of writing for people who are blind that uses raised dots as letters and numbers to be read with the fingertips: **Instead of using their eyes to read printing, people who are blind use their fingers to read** *Braille.*

bound

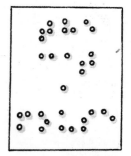

Braille

a	add	ŏŏ	took
ā	ace	ōō	pool
â	care	u	up
ä	palm	û	burn
e	end	yōō	fuse
ē	equal	oi	oil
i	it	ou	pout
ī	ice	ng	ring
o	odd	th	thin
ō	open	th	this
ô	order	zh	vision

ə = { a in *above* e in *sicken*
      i in *possible*
      o in *melon* u in *circus* }

burrow

canoe

brass [bras] *n. (pl.)* Musical instruments, such as a trumpet, that are made out of metal and that give a loud sound when blown.

bron·co·bust·er [brong′kō·bus′tər] *n.* A person who rides wild horses or bulls: *Broncobusters* **may get hurt when they ride wild horses.**

buck·skin [buk′skin′] *n.* A soft material made from the skin of deer or sheep: **My uncle has a beautiful jacket made of** *buckskin.*

bur·row [bûr′ō] *v.* **bur·rowed, bur·row·ing** To dig or hide in a hole: **I watch my hamster** *burrow* **into the leaves to make a warm nest.**

but·ler [but′lər] *n.* A person who works as the head servant of a house.

C

ca·noe [kə·nōō] *v.* **ca·noed, ca·noe·ing** To ride in a *canoe,* which is a small boat for one or two people.

cat·a·logue [kat′ə·lôg′ *or* kat′ə·log′] *n.* A book that lists things for sale: **Mr. Cortez orders many clothes from** *catalogues.*

chan·de·lier [shan′də·lir′] *n.* A lamp that hangs from the ceiling: **The** *chandelier* **over the table lit the room.**

chord [kôrd] *n.* In music, three or more sounds (notes) from a musical instrument that are played at one time: **Juan plays** *chords* **on the piano.**

cho·rus [kôr′əs] *n.* A group of singers.

clat·ter [klat′ər] *v.* **clat·tered, clat·ter·ing** To make a loud crashing or knocking noise: **The falling dishes** *clattered.*

cock·a·too [kok′ə·tōō′] *n.*
A kind of parrot:
Cockatoos **are birds
with colorful crests.**

co·coa [kō′kō] *n.* A hot
chocolate drink: **Mrs.
Brown gave us a cup of**
cocoa. syn. hot chocolate

com·mer·cial
[kə·mûr′shəl] *n.* An
advertisement on TV or
radio for the purpose of
selling something.

com·pass [kum′pəs *or*
kom′pəs] *n.* An
instrument that always
points to the north, so
people can figure out in
which direction to go.

con·ser·va·to·ry
[kən·sûr′və·tôr′ē] *n.* A
small greenhouse for
growing plants and
flowers: **Jim worked in
the** *conservatory,*
raising tulips and roses.

creek [krēk *or* krik] *n.* A
small river: **Every
summer we waded in a**
creek **by our house.**
syns. stream, brook

crin·kle [kring′kəl] *v.*
crin·kled, crin·kling
To wrinkle or put ridges
into: **She** *crinkled* **her
nose at the smelly
garbage in the alley.**

cu·ri·ous [kyŏŏr′ē·əs] *adj.*
Very interested; eager
to learn about or do
something: **The
children were** *curious* **to
hear how the story
ends.**

cus·tom [kus′təm] *n.*
Something that has been
done by a group of
people for a long time so
that it becomes part of
their ways: **A** *custom* **at
our house is to light
candles every Friday,
before sunset.**

D

deed [dēd] *n.* An action
taken; something
someone has done:
Jeff's good *deeds* **in
helping injured
animals were reported
in the local newspaper.**

dol·lop [däl′əp] *n.* A lump
or blob of something:
She spread a *dollop* **of
butter on the toast.**

cocoa The people of
Mexico gave us our word
cocoa. Chocolate is made
from *cocoa* beans.
Mexicans, who first used
chocolate, called it
chocolatl, their word for
"bitter water." Believe it or
not, it takes a lot of sugar
to make chocolate sweet!

crinkle

dollop

a	add	ŏŏ	took
ā	ace	ōō	pool
â	care	u	up
ä	palm	û	burn
e	end	yōō	fuse
ē	equal	oi	oil
i	it	ou	pout
ī	ice	ng	ring
o	odd	th	thin
ō	open	th	this
ô	order	zh	vision

ə = { a in *above* e in *sicken*
i in *possible*
o in *melon* u in *circus* }

easel Our word *easel* comes from the Dutch word *ezel*, which means "donkey." Why would a stand made to hold paintings be named after a donkey? Because a donkey is a "beast of burden" used to hold and carry loads, just as an *easel* is.

exhibition

dough [dō] *n.* A mix of flour and liquid used to make foods such as bread and muffins: **I added raisins to the *dough* before I baked the cookies.**

E

ea·sel [ē′zəl] *n.* A frame or stand used to hold the painting an artist is working on: **The artist set paper on the *easel* and started to paint.**

eld·est [el′dist] *adj.* The oldest: **Carlos is the *eldest* child in his family because all his brothers and sisters are younger than he is.**

emp·ty [emp′tē] *adj.* Not filled; holding nothing: **Waiting for dinner, Ken had an *empty* feeling in his stomach.**

en·ter·tain·ment [en′tər·tān′mənt] *n.* Something performed to interest or give pleasure to an audience: **Movies are my favorite kind of *entertainment*.**

ex·ag·ger·ate [ig·zaj′ə·rāt′] *v.* **ex·ag·ger·at·ed, ex·ag·ger·at·ing** To make something seem greater or more than it really is: **My brother *exaggerated* when he said he caught a big fish because it weighed only five pounds.**

ex·cit·ing [ik·sī′ting] *adj.* Bringing out strong feelings of interest: **The fair was very *exciting* because of the rides.**

ex·er·cise [ek′sər·sīz′] *n.* Active movement of the body to improve strength or health: **We did *exercises* in gym class to strengthen our arms.**

ex·hi·bi·tion [ek′sə·bish′ən] *n.* A showing of art: **We liked seeing the paintings at the *exhibition*.** *syn.* exhibit

ex·plore [ik·splôr′] *v.* **ex·plored, ex·plor·ing** To look around in order to find new things: **Our friends are going to *explore* the caves.**

F

fid·dle [fid'(ə)l] *n.*
Another term for a
violin: **Country music is
often played on a *fiddle*.**

fig·ure·head
[fig'yər•hed'] *n.* A
carved figure set at the
front of a sailing ship:
**The museum's old
ships had *figureheads* of
beautiful women.**

fringe [frinj] 1 *n.* A
decorative trimming of
threads hanging from an
edge. 2 *v.* To attach or
border with fringe: **Terri
helped her mom *fringe*
the tablecloth with
long, silky threads.**

frol·ic [frol'ik] *v.*
frol·icked, frol·ick·ing
To play happily about:
**The happy children
were *frolicking* in the
first snow.** *syn.* romp

G

gift [gift] *n.* Talent; a
person's inborn ability
to do something well.

gig·gle [gig'əl] *v.*
gig·gled, gig·gling To
laugh in a silly way: **All
the children started to
giggle when Joey's hat
fell in the fish tank.**

grain [grān] *n.* A tiny bit
or piece of something: **I
can't count every *grain*
of sand on this beach.**
syns. particle, speck

grand·daugh·ter
[gran(d)'dô'tər] *n.* The
daughter of a person's
son or daughter: **My
granddaughter has dark
hair and blue eyes, just
like my son has.**

grump·y [grum'pē] *adj.* In
a bad mood: **I'm *grumpy*
because I had a bad
day.** *syns.* crabby,
grouchy

H

hand·ker·chief
[hang'kər•chif] *n.* A
square piece of cloth
used to wipe the nose:
**He blew his nose with
his red *handkerchief*.**
syn. hankie

fiddle   Similar to *violin*,
fiddle comes from the name
of a Roman goddess of joy
and victory, *Vitula*. In
Latin, *Vitula* means "a
stringed instrument."
Stringed instruments were
played at festivals, thus
the meaning "joy." *Vitula*
became *violin*. In German,
it became *fiedel* and in
English, *fiddle*.

figurehead

a	add	o͝o	took
ā	ace	o͞o	pool
â	care	u	up
ä	palm	û	burn
e	end	yo͞o	fuse
ē	equal	oi	oil
i	it	ou	pout
ī	ice	ng	ring
o	odd	th	thin
ō	open	t̶h̶	this
ô	order	zh	vision

ə = { a in *above* e in *sicken*
i in *possible*
o in *melon* u in *circus* }

imitate   *Imitate* is from the Latin word *imitari*, which means "make a copy of." The words *image* and *imitate* share the base *im* meaning "likeness."

knapsack

lemming

hol·low [hol'ō] *n.* A small valley: **Ferns grow in the low ground of the hollows.**

I

im·i·tate [im'ə·tāt'] *v.* **im·i·tat·ed, im·i·tat·ing** To do something the same way as someone or something else: **When Matt was imitating Jim's laugh, we thought Jim was in the room.**

im·press [im·pres'] *v.* **im·pressed, im·press·ing** To affect someone's feelings or mind: **Juan hopes his extra work will impress his teacher.**

in·stru·ment [in'strə·mənt] *n.* A device, such as a trumpet, piano, or drum, used to make musical sounds: **Out of the many instruments Bo plays, he likes the drums best.**

isle [īl] *n.* A small island: **We paddled our canoe around the isle in the center of Beaver Lake.**

J

jew·el [jōō'əl] *n.* A gemstone of great value: **The jewel in the ring was a ruby.**

K

knap·sack [nap'sak'] *n.* A bag with shoulder straps, worn on the back: **Joe carried our picnic lunch in his knapsack.** *syn.* backpack

L

la·va·liere [läv'ə·li(ə)r'] *n.* A necklace: **Her gold lavaliere slipped off her neck during dinner and fell into her tomato soup.**

lem·ming [lem'ing] *n.* A small ratlike animal that lives in the Arctic: **Lemmings move from place to place and sometimes drown by rushing blindly into the sea.**

li·brar·y [lī'brer'ē or lī'brə•rē] *n.* A place where books are kept for reading and research: **I borrowed some books from the public** *library.*

lu·pine [loo'pin] *n.* A kind of plant related to peas and beans that has lovely flowers: **We found a blue** *lupine* **and some other wild flowers growing along the trail.**

M

mar·i·gold [mar'ə•gōld'] *n.* A yellow flower: **We planted** *marigolds* **in our flower garden.**

mar·ma·lade [mär'mə•lād] *n.* A kind of jam: **The orange** *marmalade* **Aunt June made tasted good spread on biscuits and toast.**

mast [mast] *n.* A tall pole that holds up a ship's sail: **The storm broke all the ship's** *masts,* **and the sails crashed into the sea.**

mem·o·rize [mem'ə•rīz'] *v.* **mem·o·rized, mem·o·riz·ing** To learn something by heart: **Mike is so good at** *memorizing* **songs that he can sing songs without looking at the words.** *syn.* remember

mim·ic [mim'ik] *v.* **mim·icked, mim·ick·ing** To copy or repeat what someone does or says: **The parrot was** *mimicking* **everything we said.**

mu·si·cian [myoo•zish'ən] *n.* Someone skilled in playing a musical instrument and performing music: **The** *musicians* **were playing one of their hit songs for the concert.**

N

nui·sance [n(y)oo'səns] *n.* Someone or something that bothers others: **Everyone thought Harold was a** *nuisance* **because he cried a lot.**

library   In Latin, *book* comes from the word *liber.* It also is related to the Russian word *lub,* which means "bark." Bark was one of the first materials people used to write on. *Liber* eventually became *libraria,* meaning "bookstore." In English, *library* has never meant "bookstore," but "a place where books are kept."

marigold

musician

a	add	oo	took
ā	ace	oo	pool
â	care	u	up
ä	palm	û	burn
e	end	yoo	fuse
ē	equal	oi	oil
i	it	ou	pout
ī	ice	ng	ring
o	odd	th	thin
ō	open	th	this
ô	order	zh	vision

ə = { a in *above*   e in *sicken*
      i in *possible*
      o in *melon*   u in *circus* }

orchestra *Orchestra* comes from the Greek word *orkhēstrā,* which means "a semicircular space at the front of a stage in which the chorus dances." In English it has been used to mean "the part of a theater where the musicians play." Eventually it came to mean the group of musicians itself.

percussion

O

op•er•a [op′ər•ə *or* op′rə] *n.* A play set to music in which the lines are sung: **When I attend the *opera*, I sit up front so I can better see the singers.**

or•chard [ôr′chərd] *n.* A field of trees grown for their fruit or nuts: **We went to the *orchard* to pick apples.**

or•ches•tra [ôr′kəs•trə] *n.* A group of musicians who play different instruments: **The *orchestra* received great applause when it played "The Star-Spangled Banner."**

out•doors•man [out•dôrz′man] *n., pl.* **out•doors•men** A person who enjoys spending time outdoors in nature: **We call Pedro and Luis the family *outdoorsmen* because they love to fish and hike in the mountains.**

P

per•cus•sion [pər•kush′ən] *n. (pl.)* The group of musical instruments, such as a drum, whose sound is produced by striking or hitting: **The timpani, or kettledrums, the bells, the cymbals, the triangle, and the snare drum all belong to the *percussion* section of the orchestra.**

per•form•ance [pər•fôr′məns] *n.* A show, play, or concert in front of an audience: **The audience clapped loudly at the end of the *performance*.** *syn.* act

pi•o•neer [pī′ə•nir′] *adj.* Having to do with one of the first people to settle in a particular area: **American *pioneer* families traveled west in wagons and on horseback to find new homes.**

pis·til [pis′təl] *n.* The part of a flower that produces seeds: **If you open the *pistil* of a flower, you will often see the seeds inside.**

plain [plān] *n.* A large area of almost level land without trees: **We could see for miles across the empty *plains*.** *syns.* prairie, field

pol·len [pol′ən] *n.* A powder in plants that helps seeds make new plants: ***Pollen* may be carried from one flower to another by bees.**

pon·cho [pon′chō] *n.* A rain jacket that is pulled over the head.

prai·rie [prâr′ē] *adj.* Having to do with a large grassy area without trees: ***Prairie* dogs are small animals that live in holes in the ground.**

pre·his·tor·ic [prē′his·tôr′ik] *adj.* From a time very long ago, before written history began: **Dinosaurs were *prehistoric* animals.** *syn.* ancient

pro·fes·sion·al [prə·fesh′ən·əl] *adj.* Having to do with a job that requires special training: **A mechanic's *professional* skill is needed to fix the car.**

prompt·ly [prompt′lē] *adv.* Quickly: **We were glad the fire truck arrived *promptly*.** *syn.* immediately

prow [prou] *n.* The front end of a boat or ship: **Sailors stood at the *prows* of the ships, looking ahead for signs of land.** *syn.* bow

R

rec·ol·lec·tion [rek′ə·lek′shən] *n.* Something remembered. *syns.* memory, remembrance

reed [rēd] *n.* A small, thin, flat piece of wood, metal, or plastic used as the mouthpiece or in the mouthpiece of some musical instruments, such as the clarinet: **Tracey's *reed* was broken, so no sound came out of her clarinet.**

pistil, pollen

prehistoric

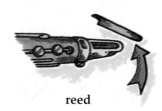

reed

a	add	o͝o	took
ā	ace	o͞o	pool
â	care	u	up
ä	palm	û	burn
e	end	yo͞o	fuse
ē	equal	oi	oil
i	it	ou	pout
ī	ice	ng	ring
o	odd	th	thin
ō	open	t͟h	this
ô	order	zh	vision

ə = { a in *above* e in *sicken*
i in *possible*
o in *melon* u in *circus* }

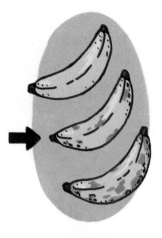

riper

rodeo

scrape

rein [rān] *v.* **reined, rein•ing** To pull back or control: **Edward *reined* in the ox and stopped plowing.**

re•tired [ri•tīrd′] *adj.* No longer working: **My mother plans to travel now that she is *retired*.**

rhythm [ri<s>th</s>′əm] *n.* Repetition of a beat played throughout a musical piece: **I tap my feet to the song's *rhythm*.**

rip•er [rīp′ər] *adj.* More ripe; fully grown or ready to eat: **Each day the tomatoes grow *riper*.** *syn.* mature

ro•de•o [rō′dē•ō *or* rō•dā′ō] *n.* A contest for people like cowhands to show their skill: **In the *rodeo*, he rode the wild horse and won a prize.**

S

sat•is•fac•tion [sat′is•fak′shən] *n.* The feeling of having what you need and want. *syns.* happiness, contentment

sci•en•tist [sī′ən•tist] *n.* A person who finds and studies information about different things: **Scientists try to learn more about dinosaurs.**

scrape [skrāp] *v.* **scraped, scrap•ing** To take something off by rubbing it with a sharp edge: **Scrape the food off the plates before washing them.**

sculpt [skulpt] *v.* **sculpted, sculpt•ing** To make or shape a statue: **The artist *sculpts* the shapes of faces in clay.** *syn.* form

set•tler [set′lər] *n.* Someone who comes to live in a new area: **Early American *settlers* came mainly from Europe.**

sha•man [shä′mən *or* shā′mən] *n.* A type of priest among Native Americans; a person who gives advice and who is greatly respected in his community.

shiv•er [shiv′ər] *v.* **shiv•ered, shiv•er•ing** To shake because of feeling cold or afraid.

short•en•ing [shôr′tən•ing] *n.* Butter or oil used in cooking.

shrill [shril] *adj.* Having a high-pitched sound: **The *shrill* sound of the whistle made us jump.**

sin•gle [sing′gəl] *adj.* Only one; one person or thing: **Not a *single* person laughed when I dropped my award.**

skil•let [skil′it] *n.* A frying pan.

splin•ter [splin′tər] *n.* A thin piece of wood split off from a larger piece: ***Splinters* from the wood got in my fingers.**

stern•ly [stûrn′lē] *adv.* Firmly; strictly: **The girl spoke to her brother so *sternly* that he began to cry.** *syn.* harshly

strings [stringz] *n. (pl.)* Musical instruments, such as the violin, that have thin wires and that are played with a bow.

stumped [stumpt] *adj. informal* Confused or without an answer: **The problem was so hard, Mom was *stumped*.**

sub•way [sub′wā′] *n.* An underground train.

T

ther•mos [thûr′məs] *n.* A bottle for keeping liquids hot or cold for several hours.

thread [thred] *n.* A very thin string of cloth: **He used *thread* to sew a tear in the old shirt.**

tin•kling [ting′kling] *adj.* Sounding soft and like a small bell.

tran•quil [trang′kwil *or* tran′kwil] *adj.* Calm and quiet: **We easily rowed the boat across the *tranquil* lake.** *syn.* peaceful

treas•ure [trezh′ər] *n.* Valuable items, such as jewels and money, which are kept stored: **The ship set sail in search of *treasure* buried deep at sea.**

tribe [trīb] *n.* A group of people who have a leader and who share beliefs: **The Seminoles are an Indian *tribe*.**

skillet

tribe *Tribe* comes from the Latin word *tribus*, meaning "division of the Roman people." Since *tri* means "three," it meant the three original tribes of Rome.

a	add	o͝o	took
ā	ace	o͞o	pool
â	care	u	up
ä	palm	û	burn
e	end	yo͞o	fuse
ē	equal	oi	oil
i	it	ou	pout
ī	ice	ng	ring
o	odd	th	thin
ō	open	th	this
ô	order	zh	vision

ə = { a in *above*   e in *sicken*
i in *possible*
o in *melon*   u in *circus* }

tropical

wilderness

woodwind

trop·i·cal [trop′i·kəl] *adj.* Like or related to a jungle or warm climate: **We enjoyed the warm weather and delicious fruit on the** *tropical* **island.**

U

u·ten·sil [yo͞o·ten′səl] *n.* A tool used to do or make something: **We keep our kitchen** *utensils* **in a drawer in the kitchen.**

V

vac·u·um [vak′yo͞o·(ə)m] *n.* **vac·u·um flask** A kind of bottle that keeps liquids hot or cold, such as a thermos bottle: **Marie kept the ice water in a tightly closed** *vacuum* **bottle to keep it cold.**

vi·sion [vizh′ən] *n.* Something imagined, as in a dream; a look into the future: **Kathy had** *visions* **of becoming a ballet dancer.**

W

war·ri·or [wôr′ē·ər *or* wor′ē·ər] *n.* A person who is or has been involved in war: **The brave** *warriors* **defended their homeland.**

wharf [(h)wôrf] *n., pl.* **wharves** or **wharfs** A dock along a shore, where boats wait to load or unload: **The fishermen steered their boats toward the** *wharves* **to unload the day's catch.**

wil·der·ness [wil′dər·nis] *n.* An area where people have not settled: **The family happily hiked and camped in the** *wilderness* **for three weeks.** *syn.* outdoors

wood·wind [wo͝od′wind′] *n.* A musical instrument, usually made of wood or metal, that you blow into or use a reed to play: **The saxophone is one of the popular** *woodwinds* **used to play jazz.**

INDEX OF
TITLES AND AUTHORS

Page numbers in light print refer to information about the author.

Acknowledgments continued

Adventures of Ali Baba Bernstein by Johanna Hurwitz, cover illustration by Gail Owens. Text copyright © 1985 by Johanna Hurwitz; cover illustration copyright © 1985 by Gail Owens. *Johnny Appleseed* by Steven Kellogg. Copyright © 1988 by Steven Kellogg.

G. P. Putnam's Sons: The Legend of the Indian Paintbrush, retold and illustrated by Tomie dePaola. Copyright © 1988 by Tomie dePaola.

Random House, Inc.: Cover illustration by Dora Leder from *Julian's Glorious Summer* by Ann Cameron. Illustration copyright © 1987 by Dora Leder.

Marian Reiner, on behalf of Myra Cohn Livingston: Untitled riddle (Retitled: "Closed, I am a Mystery") from *My Head Is Red and Other Riddle Rhymes* by Myra Cohn Livingston. Text copyright © 1990 by Myra Cohn Livingston. Published by Holiday House.

Marian Reiner, on behalf of Lillian Morrison: "Would you like?" by Lillian Morrison. Text copyright © 1983 by Lillian Morrison.

Scholastic Inc.: From *A Seed Is a Promise* by Claire Merrill. Text copyright © 1973 by Claire Merrill. Cover illustration by Margot Tomes from *Ty's One-man Band* by Mildred Pitts Walter. Illustration copyright © 1980 by Margot Tomes. Published by Four Winds Press.

Simon & Schuster Books for Young Readers, a Division of Simon & Schuster Inc.: Cover illustration from *The Keeping Quilt* by Patricia Polacco. Copyright © 1988 by Patricia Polacco.

Tumbledown Editions: "Hello Book!" by N. M. Bodecker. Text copyright © 1974 by N.M. Bodecker; text copyright © 1990 by Tumbledown Editions. Originally published by the Children's Book Council, Inc.

Viking Penguin, a division of Penguin Books USA Inc.: Miss Rumphius by Barbara Cooney. Copyright © 1982 by Barbara Cooney Porter.

Charlotte Zolotow: "People" from *All that Sunlight* by Charlotte Zolotow. Text copyright © 1967 by Charlotte Zolotow.

Photograph Credits

Key: (t) top, (b) bottom, (c) center.
William Campbell for *Time,* 122(t); William Campbell, 123(t); Christopher Vail/Black Star, 123(b); Reuters/Bettmann, 216(t); Nina Berman/Sipa Press, 216(c); Nina Berman/Sipa Press, 216(b); Ira Block/The Image Bank, 216–217(c); Flip Chalfant/The Image Bank, 217(t); Robert Berman Gallery, 316(t); Courtesy Paul Sierra, 316(b); Rick Graetz/Black Star, 316–317(c); Elisa Leonelli/Bruce Coleman, Inc., 317(t).

Illustration Credits

Key: (t) top, (b) bottom, (c) center.

Table of Contents Art
Thomas Vroman Associates, Inc., 4, 5, 6, 7, 8, 9

Unit Opener Art
Thomas Vroman Associates, Inc., 10, 11, 124, 125, 218, 219

Bookshelf Art
Thomas Vroman Associates, Inc., 12, 13, 126, 127, 220, 221

Theme Opening Art
Anni Matsick, 14, 15; Tricia Courtney, 54, 55; Eva V. Cockrille, 80, 81

Unit 2
Dora Leder, 128, 129; Gershom Griffith, 148, 149; Jane McCreary, 186, 187

Unit 3
Joe Veno, 222, 223; Lane Yerkes, 272, 273; Tom Leonard, 296, 297

Theme Wrap-up Art
Thomas Vroman Associates, Inc., 53, 79, 121, 147, 185, 215, 271, 295, 315

Connections Art
David Diaz, 112–113

Selection Art
Barbara Cooney, 16–30; Andrea Eberbach, 32–37, 313–314; Steven Kellogg, 38–52; Jan Palmer, 56–75; Karen Barber, 78; Louis Darling, 130–131, 145; Alan Tiegreen, 132–143, 146; Greg Shed, 150–167; Roberta Ludlow, 168–169; Laura C. Kelly, 170–184; Brian Deines, 188–211; Tomie dePaola, 224–253; Peggy Fortnum, 256–270; Jane Dyer, 274–288; Shelly Matheis, 292–293; Michael Stiernagle, 294; Allen Say, 298–310, 312